THREE FOR YESTERDAY

YESTERDAY

A MAGIC WOODS ADVENTURE

BY
GEORGE PATRICK LEAL

CONTENTS

6

Author's Note

Magic Woods Adventures are short books that take you deeper into the enchanting world of Magic Woods! Each one is its own unique adventure—separate from the main volumes, yet still connected in important ways. These books offer a special chance to explore certain eras and characters more deeply. Think of them as the secret paths and hidden clearings of Magic Woods, just waiting to be explored.

All good things,
G.P.L.

THREE FOR YESTERDAY

Doggie Cornelius
Munchabunch the First

ONCE UPON A TIME, there was a pair of time-traveling salamanders named "Boss" and "Shmedley." They were as unlike as winter and summer, but they made a good team. Boss was the elder of the two. He was a dusky salamander who wore old-fashioned clothes, a top hat, and spectacles. Shmedley was a blue spotted salamander. He also wore old-fashioned clothes, although they tended not to be as elaborate as Boss's outfits. Shmedley loved bird-watching and plum pudding. Together, the two salamanders piloted the *Paradox*, a time-traveling airship. They journeyed up and down the timeline of Magic Woods, investigating important historical events and taking notes. They knew quite a bit about the history of Magic Woods, but not *everything*. Sometimes they made mistakes and altered the timeline, but they didn't know they were doing that. And they certainly *tried* not to do that.

One day, Boss said, "Shmedley, our next assignment will be to see if there *was* a Doggie Cornelius Munchabunch the First. We know about the second... that's the one who appeared alongside Kitty Karate, and then *disappeared* a few months later. And, of course, we know about the third—the author of *The Complete Guide to Stinky Things in Magic Woods*. But there's evidence—well, at least, there's *rumors*—that there may have been another Doggie, *before* them. And I think I've pinpointed the exact time he appears, way back in the earlier days of Yesterday's Macaroni."

"Okay, Boss," said Shmedley, writing down an observation in his bird-watching journal.

"All right," said Boss. "Let's take the *Paradox* to the past... to the year 424 in the Fourth Age. Reckoning in Toad Cycles, of course."

"Of course," said Shmedley, putting away his journal with a sigh. He pressed some buttons on their timeship's display panel, and a moment later they were zooming through time.

☙

THEY REACHED YESTERDAY'S MACARONI in the middle of the night. It was Darkearly, the longest night of the year.

"Is this when the first Doggie appeared?" asked Shmedley.

"If my calculations are correct, yes," said Boss.

"How will we get inside the mountain?"

"Hmm," said Boss. "I guess we'll need to go down the chimney."

Shmedley flew the *Paradox* over to the mountain's massive chimney, where a steady plume of smoke was rising. He carefully lowered the ship into the dark chute.

"Go slowly now, Shmedley."

"Okay, Boss."

As they descended, Shmedley noticed the temperature was rising rapidly, and an orange-red light was growing brighter all around them. "What's that light coming from down below?" he said.

"I don't know," said Boss, peering through the cockpit windows. Suddenly, he grabbed his hat and shouted, "Great Scot! There's an actual FIRE in the fireplace! What's THAT all about? We're about to be cooked!"

"Oh," said Shmedley.

"Back it up!" cried Boss. "Back it up!"

Shmedley frantically hit some buttons, and even Boss pulled a lever or two. The *Paradox* reversed course just in time, and zoomed up out of the chimney.

"Hmm," mused Boss, adjusting his spectacles. "It seems we'll need to find another way inside."

"Agreed," said Shmedley.

Boss rubbed his chin. "Let's see if the Thingumybob can handle the front door."

(The Thingumybob was a versatile handheld device. It was made of polished brass and adorned with intricate clockwork mechanisms. Buttons, levers, dials, and switches covered its surface. This remarkable gadget could alter memories, distort time, stun enemies, rearrange probability parameters, and many other things besides).

They flew the *Paradox* around to the mountain's entrance. Shmedley opened a window and aimed the Thingumybob at the imposing front door. He adjusted a few dials and pressed a series of buttons. A spiraling beam of blue light shot out from the device, wrapping around the brass doorknob like a snake. Moments later, the door to Yesterday's Macaroni creaked open, soundlessly inviting them inside.

Carefully maneuvering the *Paradox* through the open doorway, they guided it into the cavernous interior and closed the door behind them. The ship came to rest in the shadows at the edge of the main room.

Stepping out of the *Paradox*, they surveyed their surroundings. The fireplace that had nearly consumed them stood at one end of the room. Nearby, the Darkearly Tree rose in silent splendor, its branches adorned with delicate trinkets that twinkled faintly in the firelight.

"How pretty!" whispered Shmedley. "Do you think there are any wild bird species in that tree?"

"I doubt it," said Boss.

"Not even a beige bunting?"

"Not even that."

Boss checked his pocket watch and frowned. "Now, according to my calculations, the first Doggie should be appearing soon... if, indeed, he appears at all."

They waited and waited, looking around the room, but nothing happened.

Boss sighed. "I guess there never WAS a Doggie Cornelius Munchabunch the First."

But then Shmedley saw a little face under the tree, popping up from behind a stack of presents. It was a cute little hound dog puppy.

Shmedley poked Boss excitedly.

Boss frowned. "Why are you poking me?"

Shmedley pointed under the tree. "Look! Isn't that maybe him?"

Boss adjusted his glasses. "Oh my goodness!" he whispered. "I think you're right. That IS Doggie Cornelius Munchabunch the First. He looks just like the other ones—if we can believe the album cover art and the author photo."

"I wonder what happens to him?" said Shmedley.

"Well, presumably, he disappears or dies at some point," answered Boss. "There's no official record of him... he must not have lasted very long."

Shmedley frowned. "Aw. Poor thing. He's cute! Couldn't we keep him, if he's just gonna die or disappear anyways?"

"No," said Boss firmly. "That probably wouldn't be a good idea."

All of a sudden, from behind, they heard a loud voice. "Seaweed and sassafras! It's the Toad Instigators! They dared to come back!"

Boss and Shmedley whipped around. They saw Mr. Constrictor, a big dusty pink snake with weird white things where his eyes should have been. Behind him stood a small hippo with three bellybuttons, a crimson ape in valentine overalls, and a crimson *bear* in valentine overalls.

"Why, I do believe that's four of the Town Elders!" said Boss excitedly.

"Who are you calling *elders*?" huffed Mr. Constrictor. "We're the Youth Brigade!"

"I see," said Boss. "My apologies. Allow us to introduce ourselves—"

"We already know who you are," said Mr. Constrictor angrily. "You're the original Toad Instigators!

"Why do you call us *toad instigators*?" asked Shmedley.

"You're the ones who got the toads all riled up, way back when!" said Mr. Constrictor. "Now they invade our town twice a month. We've been waiting for you to return, so we could toss you into the dungeons!"

Love Bear frowned. "But we don't *have* dungeons."

"Well, we'll *make* some for these two slippery characters," said Mr. Constrictor.

"We never did anything with *toads*," said Shmedley, offended. "Just because we're amphibians doesn't mean we consort with *toads* and their ilk. And we're not *that* slippery."

Boss nodded suddenly. "Ah, Shmedley, I think I know what's happening. Perhaps we go to *their* past at some point in *our* future, and inadvertently cause some sort of toad trouble."

"What in the name of tarnation are you talking about?" said Mr. Constrictor.

While this was happening, the first Doggie snuck over to see what was going on. He watched them all with his tail wagging, and listened carefully to everything they said.

Boss turned to Shmedley. "Use the Thingumybob and freeze them for a minute so we can escape to the *Paradox*. Also: scramble their brains a little."

Mr. Constrictor raised himself to his full height. "Scramble our brains!?"

Shmedley reached into his pocket... and gasped. "Oh, no," he said. "It's not there, Boss. I must have dropped it."

"Oh boy," said Boss. "We're in trouble."

"You two have a lot of explaining to do," said Mr. Constrictor.

"Maybe we should use the Orb on them," Love Ape suggested.

Shmedley swallowed nervously. "The *orb*? What's that?"

"An orb is a sort of sphere," said Boss.

"I *know*," said Shmedley. "But what's it gonna *do* to us?"

"You two are gonna answer for why you caused the toads to invade our town," said Mr. Constrictor menacingly.

All of a sudden, a burst of brilliant yellow light erupted from the shadows, striking the Town Elders—er, the Youth Brigade— and freezing them in place. Their movements halted mid-step, their faces locked in comical expressions of surprise.

Shmedley and Boss whirled around, seeking the source of the blast. To their utter astonishment, they saw Doggie standing there, gripping the Thingumybob with a mix of pride and uncertainty.

"Did I do the right thing?" Doggie asked, his ears slightly lowered as though bracing for a reprimand.

"Yes, you did!" Boss exclaimed, his voice filled with relief, though his eyes were wide with surprise. "You saved us!"

"Uh... can I have my Thingumybob back now?" Shmedley asked.

"Okay, here you go," said Doggie cheerfully, handing over the gadget without hesitation. Shmedley took it gingerly, inspecting the device as though expecting it to have transformed in Doggie's paws.

"I... I don't understand," said Shmedley. He tilted his head, studying Doggie with newfound curiosity. "How in the world did you manage to use it correctly? You've never even handled it before."

Doggie shrugged. "I just kind of... thought about what needed to happen, and pressed some buttons, and then it happened. Is that bad?"

Boss's eyes lit up. "Fascinating! The Thingumybob must have responded to his intentions through some form of cognitive synchronization. The device likely interpreted his mental directive and translated it into action. A subconscious resonance with its operational core, perhaps... or even a latent psychic interface embedded in the design!"

Shmedley puffed out his chest. "Well, of *course* it's embedded. I designed it that way."

Boss turned, peering at Shmedley over his spectacles. "You did?"

"I purposefully added micro-synchronizers into the interface to resonate with the neural oscillations of the operator," Shmedley explained. "User intention is part of what makes the Thingumybob work." He frowned, glancing sidelong at Doggie. "But still... it should have been impossible for him to work it successfully using ONLY intention."

Boss nodded. "Quite extraordinary, really. But, I suspect it only worked because Doggie's cognitive state at that precise moment was unclouded by prior experience—essentially he was a blank slate, and this allowed the device's internal logic to override its usual safeguards. The odds of replicating such a phenomenon are vanishingly small."

"Oh," said Doggie.

Boss bowed. "Well, we must be on our way. It was a pleasure to meet you, Mr. Doggie Cornelius Munchabunch the First."

Doggie frowned. "I'm not the *first*... my name's just Doggie Cornelius Munchabunch." Then his eyes widened. "OH! Wait! If I'm the *first*, does that means I'm going to have a son who will be the *second*? Am I going to get married and have kids?"

"Um," said Boss.

Doggie's eyes sparkled, reflecting the lights of the Darkearly Tree. "I can't wait to see who I marry and have kids with. Oh, that will be so fun, to fall in love someday!"

Shmedley smiled. "Aw. He's cute, Boss."

Boss rolled his eyes. "Goodbye, Mr. Munchabunch."

"Oh, um, goodbye, I guess," said Doggie sadly.

The salamanders walked away. Shmedley's eyes lit up as he spotted candy canes dangling temptingly from the branches of the Darkearly Tree. "Boss, can we grab one of those candy canes?" he asked.

Boss adjusted his spectacles and regarded the tree for a moment, his mind calculating the risks. "Get two," he said at last. "But make it quick!"

"Okay!" Shmedley replied. He darted toward the Darkearly Tree and leapt onto the lowest branch, gripping it tightly with his small hands and kicking his legs to hoist himself up. Many of the branches had sticky pine pitch on them. "Ick," he muttered under his breath, as he tried to wipe pitch from his fingers.

From below, Boss kept a sharp eye on the frozen Youth Brigade. "Hurry, Shmedley!" he called. The Brigade's frozen forms seemed to shift ever so slightly—an eye twitching here, a finger flexing there. Time was slipping away.

"I'm trying!" said Shmedley, his arms straining as he reached for another branch. He paused for a moment, catching his breath, and glanced down. The sight made his stomach flip—he was higher than he'd realized, and the ground seemed unnervingly far below.

"Don't look down, Shmedley!" said Boss.

With a deep breath, Shmedley pressed on, his hand finally closing around one candy cane, then another. He grinned. "Got them!" he called.

"Good, now get down—quickly!" said Boss, his gaze darting back to the Youth Brigade. The crimson ape had tilted its head ever so slightly. The freezing spell was rapidly wearing off.

Shmedley swung his legs over the branch and began his descent, every step down more precarious than the climb up, as he was now holding two large candy canes in his arms. The sticky pitch coated his fingers and his clothes, and twice he nearly lost his footing. "Almost there," he whispered to himself, clutching the candy canes like they were priceless relics.

Finally, with one last hop, he landed back on solid ground, the candy canes in hand and his heart pounding like a drum.

Then he and Boss ran to the *Paradox*. They rushed into the cockpit and sat at their seats. They pressed some glowing buttons, pulled a couple of levers, and adjusted a few dials. In an instant, the engines roared to life, and a powerful hum filled the cockpit. The *Paradox* lifted effortlessly from the ground and accelerated through a swirling vortex of light and shadow. Time itself unraveled and rewove around them, drawing them forward into their next adventure.

"So, our mission was a success," said Boss grandly. "We found out there WAS a first Doggie."

"And we almost got in trouble," said Shmedley.

"Yes, but we didn't. We escaped."

"Because of Doggie," said Shmedley. "I wish we could have thanked him."

All of a sudden, they heard a voice behind them say, "You're welcome!"

They turned to find Doggie himself standing there, grinning widely.

CHAPTER 2

The Ways of a Time Traveler

"HOW—WHAT—WHEN—" BOSS spluttered, gaping at Doggie.

Doggie wagged his tail eagerly, his bright eyes darting around the cockpit as he took in every detail. The cockpit was a dazzling display of magical technology, from colorful buttons that blinked and pulsed in mesmerizing patterns to levers of varying sizes— some sleek and metallic, others covered in rubbery grips. Gears clicked and whirred behind transparent panels, and an intricate display of readouts and indicators glowed with numbers and symbols. The control console was a patchwork of flashing lights, with some dials spinning and others remaining still.

"This is such a cool vehicle!" said Doggie, his voice filled with awe. "Look at all the buttons and levers and gears and indicators! And these readouts... what's a quantum flux? Everything is so high-tech and amazing! Oh, I would love to have a machine like this someday!"

"No," said Boss. "Just... no. You can't be here."

"But I really want to come with you guys!" said Doggie. "I saw your ship and wanted to find out more. Where do you come from? Are you lizard wizards from the future?"

"We're not *lizards*," huffed Shmedley. "We're not reptiles at all. We're amphibians."

"Oh," said Doggie. "Okay. Are you *amphibian* wizards from the future?"

"No," said Shmedley. "We're just time travelers from the future." He frowned. "Well, sort of. An *alternate* future..."

"THAT IS SO COOL!" said Doggie. "I'm so excited! Where are we going next?"

"Well, it's too late for us to change course now," said Boss, glancing at a monitor. "But after *this* adventure, we're going to have to bring you back where you belong."

Doggie put his tail between his legs and made big sad puppy dog eyes at them.

"Aw," said Shmedley. "He looks so sad and cute."

"He's doing that on purpose," said Boss. "To tug at your heartstrings."

"Is it working?" asked Doggie.

"Yes," gushed Shmedley.

"That's enough of that," said Boss. "Now, we're about to head to the Third Age of this world, right before the Great War started. And Mr. Cornelius Munchabunch, you are going to stay in the *Paradox* while we do our work."

"Oh, come on!" said Doggie. "Please, let me go outside with you. I wanna explore!"

"No, it'll be too dangerous," said Boss. "For you, and for the timeline. You are unschooled in the ways of a time traveler."

"But if I stay inside the *Paradox*, I might accidentally press a bunch of buttons or bump a lever," said Doggie craftily.

Boss blanched. "Okay, fine, you're coming outside with us."

"Hooray!" said Doggie.

"Now, we're going to a point in time just before the Great War started. We're hoping to catch a glimpse of Serv, the Spirit in the Shadows."

"Oooh, who's that?" asked Doggie.

"He is nothing more nor less than the supreme evil of this world," answered Boss.

"Oh," said Doggie. "Well, why do we want to see THAT guy?"

Shmedley looked at Boss curiously. "Yeah, Boss, why do we want to see HIM?"

"Why, for research purposes, of course! We want to see what he looks like in his fair form. The Spirit in the Shadows—or

Discord, if you prefer his original name—appeared as a handsome fellow named *Serv*. He walked the earth and tricked folk into doing what he wanted. He influenced them with his good looks."

"Kind of like *me* tricking *you* by being extra cute a couple of minutes ago?" said Doggie.

"Yes," said Boss. He looked at the monitor again. "Now, we're almost there. Listen to everything we say, and follow our instructions, Mr. Munchabunch."

"I will," said Doggie. His eyes grew dreamy and faraway. "Ooh, I wonder if I'm going to meet my future wife on this trip? Oh, that'd be so exciting! What if this is where I meet the love of my life?"

"You're not going to meet the love of your life 3200 years in the past, trust me," said Boss. "There weren't even any Talking Animals back then."

"Oh," said Doggie. "Well, maybe on the NEXT adventure!"

"There will be no *next* adventure for you," said Boss.

Shmedley pressed a series of glowing buttons. The *Paradox* hummed in response, shifting and adjusting slightly as it exited the timestream. With a soft whirring sound, the landing gears extended, and the *Paradox* settled gently in a meadow. A dusty dirt road wound its way along the edge of the meadow, disappearing into the faraway hills. They could see a schoolhouse in the distance.

"Okay," said Boss, scanning the landscape through the window. "Sometime in this period, Serv comes to Colleenia. Let's watch for him on the path."

They stepped out of the machine and Boss said, "Now, Mr. Munchabunch. Listen to me..."

"Okay!" said Doggie, but he was busy sniffing the flowers and dirt and grass. He didn't even look at Boss.

"Stop sniffing everything!" Boss commanded.

Doggie shrugged. "I'm a dog. That's what we do. I like all these new smells. I'm exploring!"

"Yes," said Boss. "But listen—if you go to the past and disturb *anything,* it could... well, it could damage the future and destroy this whole world!"

Doggie stopped sniffing and frowned at Boss. "Whoa. Then, why do *you* guys do it?"

"I don't know," admitted Shmedley.

"Because we *have* to," said Boss, standing tall. "It's our destiny. Now, you don't want to damage or change anything in the past."

"Okay," said Doggie, listening now.

"If you even step on a butterfly, you could alter the entire course of the future. So watch what you do, and tread carefully. Understood?"

Doggie frowned. "I thought you said to make sure we don't step on anything?"

"Yes," said Boss. "That's EXACTLY what I said."

Doggie pointed at Boss's feet. "Well, what about that stinkbug you're standing on?"

"What?" said Boss, stepping to the side and looking down. "Oh, dear..." Sure enough, he had stepped on a stinkbug. A couple of its legs were squashed, and one wing was broken, and its guts were... well, let's just say, it didn't look good for this little critter.

"Oh dear," said Boss. "Well, hopefully, one little random stinkbug won't matter in the grand scheme of things."

"But I thought you said even one dead butterfly could destroy the future," said Doggie.

"Yes, well..."

Everyone stood silent a moment. Then Doggie heard a faraway voice on the breeze, barely audible: *"Who's the Special Boo?"*

Before Doggie could say anything, Shmedley stiffened, staring down the dirt road. "Boss, there's someone coming..."

Boss adjusted his glasses and squinted into the distance. "Maybe it's Serv," he said.

"No," said Shmedley, peering through binoculars. "It looks like a Meemie girl, but she doesn't have wings. She's wearing a kind of raggedy dress... and she's coming right towards us!"

"Oh dear," said Boss. "We need to get out of here before she sees us!"

"What should we do about the stinkbug?" asked Doggie.

"I guess we'll just leave it, and hopefully it won't die," said Boss. "And if it *does,* hopefully its death won't change the future *too* much."

They clambered back into the *Paradox,* the metal ramp closing behind them with a soft hiss. With a flick of switches and the press of buttons, the engines came to life, sending vibrations thrumming through the entire vessel. In an instant, the *Paradox* lifted smoothly off the ground, leaving a whirl of dust and loose leaves swirling in its wake. The meadow vanished beneath them as the ship tilted upward and shot forward. They broke through the barriers of space and time, zooming away into the swirling timestream.

The little girl walking up the road was named "Lila." Luckily, she had been too busy looking down and didn't notice their timeship as it sped away. But she DID notice the wounded stinkbug on the ground. "Oh!" she said. "Poor thing." She picked him up and brought him back to her room to take care of him. She named him "Chester."

(And Chester was actually Mandaloko—the Creator of Magic Woods—in stinkbug form, so it's a good thing she saved his life!)

CHAPTER 3

Plum Pudding Interlude

BRILLIANT ARCS OF LIGHT surrounded the *Paradox* as it sped through the timestream, streaks of color twisting and dancing like liquid rainbows. The ship soared through the endless current, cutting effortlessly through the vortex, as they raced onward to their next destination.

On board the *Paradox*, Boss said, "I feel bad about that stinkbug. But I'm sure he wasn't an important one."

"*Are* there important stinkbugs?" Shmedley wondered.

"Probably not," said Boss.

"So, where are we going to now?" asked Doggie.

"We need to take you back to your time and your home," said Boss.

"Actually, Boss," said Shmedley, "we're headed back to OUR home right now. I had already pre-programmed the coordinates. And then we'll need a little more azidozide before we can jump back to Doggie's time."

"Oh dear. Alright. Well, then, first we're going to Laterberry— that's where we store our azidozide."

"What's azidozide?" asked Doggie.

"It's a rare substance that powers our time circuits. It was once mined in Penelopolee."

"*Penelopolee!*" sang Doggie. "That's a fun name!"

"Indeed. We snagged some raw azidozide from there and then, but we also managed to filch a bunch from someone named Mr. Tomfoolery."

"Ooh!" said Doggie. "Mr. Tomfoolery. He sounds like a fun guy! Can I meet him? Maybe we'll become best friends, and then maybe he'll be the best man at my wedding... when I finally get married to the love of my life!" He wagged his tail. "Maybe I'll meet her in Laterberry!"

"Laterberry doesn't have any people in it," said Boss curtly.

"Oh," said Doggie. "Does it have any dogs?"

"No, it doesn't have any *anything*," said Boss. "It's a city on the verge of tomorrow. It's a city that will never come to be... but if it HAD come to be, Shmedley and I would have been two of its citizens."

"That's weird," said Doggie.

"I agree," said Shmedley.

☙

AT LAST THEY CAME to Laterberry, a bluish mountain hidden in a juniper forest. They parked the *Paradox* and went inside. The mountain was empty and cold, although there was a strange sense that someone was always lurking around the next corner.

"This place is kind of creepy," said Doggie, looking around the empty rooms. "But also kind of sad."

"It's a town that never actually comes to be," said Shmedley. His voice was heavy with a sadness Doggie hadn't heard before. "Me and Boss *would* have been from this town, *if* it had ever come to be."

"Er," said Doggie. "But you ARE here. You exist."

Shmedley shrugged. "In a way. But we're not REALLY part of the world. We're just observers, drifting through time, watching events unfold but never truly being part of them." He paused, his voice thick with wistfulness. "We don't have our own story, not really. We're like ghosts, never leaving a mark, never having a life of our own."

"Now, Shmedley," said Boss, not unkindly. "We mustn't get TOO sentimental. Such is the life of a time traveler."

Shmedley nodded. "Yes, Boss."

They led Doggie to a seemingly ordinary section of wall. With a knowing smile, Boss pressed his hand against a knot in the wood, and a hidden panel slid aside, revealing a narrow passageway. A series of magical oil lamps flared into life.

"Come on," Shmedley whispered excitedly, his blue skin gleaming in the warm lamplight. Doggie followed them down the passage, his eyes wide with curiosity. The passage opened into a set of adjoining little dens, each one filled with stacks of papers, leather-bound journals, and shelves lined with books. The air smelled of ink and parchment. "This is where we keep our most important research," Boss explained, adjusting his spectacles.

"And our azidozide," said Shmedley, grabbing two vials of the strange liquid metal from a hidden cupboard.

"Shmedley, why don't you see if you can procure some food," said Boss, shuffling through some papers.

"Okay, Boss."

"Please *try* not to think of plum pudding," said Boss. "Maybe you could think of something that the dog would like as well."

"Okay," said Shmedley.

Doggie watched as Shmedley adjusted the possibility parameters on the Thingumybob and concentrated.

POP! Three bowls of plum pudding appeared.

"Shmedley," said Boss wearily.

"Sorry, Boss, it's just what I always think of." Shmedley offered a bowl to Doggie. "You want some?"

Doggie shook his head, turning up his nose at the smell. "No, that's okay. I don't feel very hungry right now."

"Well, you gotta eat *something*," said Shmedley. "You haven't even had any food yet in your life!"

"Hmm," said Doggie. "I guess that's right."

"What do you want your first food to be?" asked Shmedley. "Maybe you could have Boss's candy cane…"

"Hey!" said Boss, looking up from his plum pudding. "I *want* that candy cane!"

Shmedley smiled at Doggie. "Well, you can have *my* candy cane, if you'd like."

"Oh, no thanks," said Doggie. "I don't think my first food should be a dessert. I should eat something healthy for me first. So, I'll just wait. I don't mind."

After the salamanders finished their pudding, Doggie joined them back on the *Paradox*. Shmedley got to work refilling the time travel cells with azidozide. He placed protective goggles over his eyes and donned a pair of rubber gloves. Doggie watched in fascination. "Why do you have to do that?" he asked.

"Because," said Shmedley. "Azidozide can be very dangerous if handled improperly. Each time cell needs to be filled with a steady, precise flow." Shmedley kept his hand as steady as possible as he poured the viscous liquid metal from a special anti-reaction container. The faint blue vapor rising from the liquid made Doggie's nose tingle. Shmedley managed to finish the job without a hitch, resealing the cells with a quick twist and securing them into place with heavy brass clasps.

Doggie wagged his tail excitedly. "You guys are so cool! I can't wait to learn more about the ways of a time traveler."

"That shan't happen," said Boss. "We are going to take you back home now, Mr. Munchabunch."

"Please, can I stay with you guys?" asked Doggie, trying his hardest to look as cute as possible. "You seem like you have a lot of fun! And I'd be a good companion, I promise."

"He IS a good companion," said Shmedley. "And if he's just destined to disappear anyways..."

Doggie frowned. "What do you mean, *disappear*?"

Boss peered at him over the rims of his spectacles. "You're one of the unfortunate Talking Animals—of which there are far too many, alas!—who mysteriously disappear. We still haven't been able to figure out what happens to those who vanish. All we know is that: in this world, Talking Animals *appear* from nowhere... and sometimes, when no one is looking, they *disappear*."

Doggie clutched at the front of Boss's suit. "I don't wanna disappear! Please let me stay with you guys! Please?"

"Sorry," said Boss.

"But how am I gonna meet the love of my life, and have fun adventures, and make best friends, and eat my first food, if I disappear?" said Doggie. "There's so much I want to see and do and smell and taste and feel!"

In the silence that followed, he heard that faraway voice again: *"Who's the Special Boo?"* But he decided not to say anything, because he could sense that Boss and Shmedley were considering letting him stay.

Shmedley looked at Boss. "Well, why *can't* he stay with us?"

Boss sighed. "I *suppose* if he was just going to disappear anyways, we might as well bring him with us. At least for a time."

"Yay!" said Doggie, bouncing with joy. "I'm a true-blue Time Traveler, now!"

"Not yet," said Boss sternly. "Not by a long shot, my boy."

Onyx & Lubtassium

BOSS SAID, "OUR NEXT adventure is to see how Reversa the sorceress managed to create a towering onyx castle and an army of living rock soldiers."

"Ooh!" said Doggie. "That sounds really interesting. And maybe a little scary."

"Yes," agreed Boss. "This mission might actually be a bit TOO scary for you, Mr. Munchabunch. You're not quite up for this challenge yet. I think you should stay on board the *Paradox* while we do the investigating."

"Oh," said Doggie dejectedly. "But I'd like to come on the adventure, too."

"Well, we need someone to guard the *Paradox*," said Boss. "Versa was a very dangerous Meemie, and Reversa—who was her evil double—was even worse. Possibly."

"How can someone evil have an evil double?" asked Doggie. "Wouldn't they be *good?*"

"Well, yes, in *theory*," said Boss. "But Versa's double came out of Echo Lake, which means it's an echo of her, a reflection, rather then her exact opposite."

"So, evil, but in a different way?" said Doggie.

"Precisely!" said Boss. "Anyhow, it's long been a mystery how Reversa managed to make a formidable castle out of onyx, and how she managed to bring rock soldiers to life. We aim to find out how she did both. Now, let's go!"

Shmedley pulled a series of levers and pressed several buttons, and with a soft hum, the *Paradox* shuddered and hurtled backward through the timestream. They emerged at the dawn of the Fourth Age. The *Paradox* descended gracefully into the swampy reaches of Fenmire, near the glistening expanse of Echo Lake. Mist curled and drifted through the air, and the scent of wet leaves and moss filled their nostrils as they stepped out of the ship.

Shmedley's ears perked up as he scanned the surroundings. "Ooh, I thought I heard a beige bunting!" he exclaimed, eyes wide with excitement.

Boss let out a long-suffering sigh. "Yes, quite possibly you did. Seeing as they are among the most common bird species in Magic Woods. And among the blandest, I'd say."

Shmedley turned to Doggie, his enthusiasm undampened. "Beige buntings are my favorite kind of bird!" he said, pulling his battered bird-watching journal from his jacket pocket. He flipped it open, eagerly jotting down the observation. Just as he finished, his head snapped up. "Oooh! Listen! I hear some starlings, and... oh, that might be a song sparrow... and a robin!"

Boss turned to Doggie. "As you can see, Shmedley fancies himself an amateur ornithologist."

"What does that mean?" asked Doggie.

"He studies birds. And likes them."

Shmedley looked up from his journal. "I've always wanted to see the birds that live in BirdSanktuary-land."

"Well, then, why don't we go there?" asked Doggie.

Shmedley looked at Boss hopefully.

"There's no reason to," answered Boss. "Nothing ever happened in BirdSanktuary-land. It was a sanctuary, as the name indicates. A place for *wild* birds—not for Stick People or Slurkwyrms or Bridge Trolls or Talking Animals or Meemies, even. No one ever lived there. So, there's no reason to explore it. Nothing of historical importance ever happened there."

"But Shmedley *wants* to go!" said Doggie.

"Well, *perhaps* we'll find time between missions to visit, briefly, one day," said Boss, turning abruptly and scanning the horizon.

Shmedley smiled sadly at Doggie. "He's been saying that for a long time," he whispered. "We'll probably *never* go. But a salamander can dream, can't he?"

Doggie patted his shoulder in sympathy.

"Okay," said Boss, turning back to them. "We've arrived a few hours before Reversa is brought to life." He pointed a finger at Doggie. "You will stay with the *Paradox*. And guard it."

"Okay," said Doggie glumly.

Shmedley and Boss crept quietly through the dense, misty swamps of Fenmire, their feet squelching softly in the muck. They moved cautiously. As they approached the clearing where the onyx castle would soon stand, Boss motioned for Shmedley to stop. He leaned in and whispered, "Now, according to my research, this is the exact moment when the castle was created."

Hearts pounding with anticipation, they raised their binoculars and peered through the leafy undergrowth. There, in the heart of the clearing, stood a figure: a Meemie with wild, tangled hair and eyes that sparkled with fire. She wore the fabled Crown of Creation on her forehead. The crystal at the front of the crown blazed with a vivid red light, casting eerie reflections across the swamp.

"I believe that's Versa," Boss whispered in awe.

Versa moved with a commanding presence, her every gesture radiating raw magical energy. She approached a jagged mound of black volcanic rock, her hands trembling slightly as she reached out. The red light from the crystal intensified, bathing the entire area in a crimson glow. Versa touched the rock pile, and the Crown's magic surged to life. A crackling hum filled the air as the volcanic rock twisted and reshaped itself, growing and expanding with astonishing speed. Before Shmedley and Boss's eyes, the pile transformed into a towering onyx castle, its black spires piercing the sky, and its polished walls gleaming darkly under the shimmering light of the Crown.

"Well!" said Boss. "That explains a great deal. It was *Versa* who created the castle, using the Crown. Interesting."

"But doesn't *Reversa* end up living in the castle?" asked Shmedley.

"Yes. Hmm. I wonder why. And how. And when."

Suddenly, they heard a noise in the bushes behind them. Shmedley shivered with fear and excitement. "Maybe it's a yellow-headed newtcatcher!" he said.

But then they saw a little flash of brown and white, and they realized it was Doggie.

"Mr. Munchabunch!" said Boss sharply.

"Sorry," said Doggie, stepping out of the bushes. He looked at them sheepishly. "I just got scared waiting in the *Paradox*. Plus, I wanted to see what was going on."

"You thought you were scared *there*?" said Boss. "You'll be more scared *here*. You do NOT want to mess with Versa. Now, just go back and wait in the *Paradox*. After you've learned a few more skills and techniques and strategems, and gotten a little wiser, maybe you can come with us when we investigate evildoers. But for right now, it's in your best interest to stay put."

"Okay," said Doggie with a sigh, and he slunk dejectedly back to the *Paradox*.

Boss spoke to Shmedley. "Well, let's get closer. We gotta find out how Versa—or Reversa—brings those stone soldiers to life."

They crept cautiously to the castle. Shadows seemed to pool at the base of the structure, and the air was thick with an unnatural stillness. Finding an open doorway on the side, they slipped inside. Their breath was visible in the frigid chill of the interior. The castle's walls glistened in the dim light filtering in from the narrow windows. It was cold enough to make a shiver run down Shmedley's spine.

"Sometimes I hate being cold-blooded," he lamented, pulling his coat around him tightly.

They moved silently through the echoing halls. As they neared the center courtyard, they paused, hearing the muffled sound of Versa's voice. She was murmuring strange incantations.

Peeking carefully around a massive stone column, they saw Versa standing in the center of the courtyard. Her wild hair swayed slightly in the currents of magic swirling around her, and the Crown of Creation on her head pulsed with red light. Before her lay a pile of dull gray stones. Versa raised her hands, and the crystal on the Crown flared, sending crimson energy crackling through the air. The stones began to tremble and shift, melding together and reforming into the shapes of imposing stone soldiers, each one poised as if ready for battle.

"Look, Shmedley!" Boss whispered, barely containing his excitement. "Look at that! She's making them! She's creating the stone soldiers right before our eyes!"

"Wow," Shmedley murmured, his voice full of fear.

They watched as Versa tried several dark spells to animate the newly formed soldiers, her hands weaving through the air and her voice growing more forceful with each failed attempt. The soldiers remained motionless. With a final, exasperated cry, Versa gave up. Her wings unfurled, and she lifted off the ground and flew away, vanishing into the distance.

"So, *Versa* didn't bring them to life," said Boss. "I wonder how they were brought to life at all?"

"Is she maybe coming back?" asked Shmedley.

"No, Shmedley. If my calculations are right, she's going to look into Echo Lake in a few minutes, and that's how Reversa is created. And after that, Versa just leaves this land forever. So, somehow, it's *Reversa* who brings the Rock People to life. And yet, without the aid of the Crown of Life. I wonder how?"

They heard a noise behind them. Shmedley reached into his coat for the Thingumybob, but then they saw it was only Doggie, peeking at them from around a corner.

Boss put his hands on his hips. "Mr. Munchabunch, really!"

"I'm sorry," said Doggie. "I just... I just wanted to know... I just really want to see what's going on. I think the best way for me to learn to be brave and smart is to actually *have* adventures!"

"Mr. Munchabunch, I am going to insist that you obey me, as the captain of the *Paradox*," said Boss sternly. "Stay where I tell you to stay!"

"All right," said Doggie, and he turned to leave.

"Actually," said Boss, "Shmedley and I will walk you back to the ship, to make sure you *really* go."

"Okay," said Doggie dejectedly.

They made their way back through the cold, echoing halls of the castle, guiding Doggie along the swampy forest paths until they returned him safely to the ship. With Doggie settled, Boss and Shmedley ventured back into the castle, moving with quiet steps through shadowy corridors until they reached the central courtyard. Versa was nowhere to be seen, but her handiwork was still there: an imposing army of stone soldiers, around three dozen in all.

"Those are the Rock People, for sure," Boss murmured, his eyes narrowing as he studied them.

"Seems that way," said Shmedley.

"But how did she bring them to life?" Boss wondered aloud.

Shmedley thought carefully. "What did she make them out of? Maybe there's something unique in the stone itself."

"Excellent thinking, Shmedley!" Boss's face lit up. "Get a reading with the Thingumybob."

Shmedley adjusted several dials on the mysterious device, pressing a few buttons before pointing it at one of the Rock People. A thin beam of light flickered over the stone soldier. Boss leaned close to the Thingumybob to see the reading. His face broke into a satisfied grin. "A-ha! Just as I thought. Versa built these soldiers out of lubtassium."

"Lubtassium?" Shmedley echoed, puzzled.

"Yes, an elusive substance once combined with quicksilver and coaxed into a living metal, back in the days of Korvad the Crimson King." Boss rubbed his chin thoughtfully. "It has peculiar properties—a latent energy that, when activated, can mimic life itself. I'd wager Reversa is able to awaken those living qualities and infuse them with her dark will. A grim form of life... if you can even call it life."

A sudden voice behind them interrupted. "Sounds like a wonderful idea! Thank you for the insight."

They whirled around to see Reversa standing there, her eyes gleaming in triumph.

Reversa's Dungeon

"YIKES!" SHMEDLEY GASPED, STUMBLING back a step.

Reversa's lips curled into a wry smile. "I had no idea lubtassium held such potential. Thanks for the information."

Before Boss and Shmedley could react, Reversa raised her hands and cast a dark spell, throwing them backward into the cold wall. The Thingumybob clattered from Shmedley's hands, landing on the stone floor. With a triumphant smirk, Reversa bent down, scooping up the curious device and examining it with interest.

"Ohhh, now this looks intriguing," she mused, turning it over in her hands. Her wild eyes gleamed with curiosity. "Although it doesn't seem to rely on Deep Magic... how fascinating. A combination of Easy Magic and technology, yes?" She glanced at them, her eyebrows raised.

Shmedley and Boss exchanged a wary glance but remained silent.

Reversa shrugged indifferently. "Well, no matter. I'll soon test it for its properties." Her gaze sharpened, and she tilted her head, a cruel smile spreading across her face. "Now, what should I do with the two of you?"

Shmedley swallowed nervously. "Let us go?"

Reversa tapped her chin, pretending to consider. "No, I think not. I've never had Talking Animals as guests before. How novel. I have so many questions, you see. So, you'll be my prisoners... until I get bored of you."

With a flick of her wrist, she conjured chains of shadow that bound them, dragging them down to the dark, foreboding dungeons in the castle's basement. There, she shoved them into a dank cell, the bars narrow and iron-cold. The only source of light was a single, sputtering torch, casting flickering shadows across the damp, stone walls.

"We're in a real pickle now, Boss," said Shmedley.

"Indeed," said Boss.

Moments later, the sound of footsteps echoed down the stone stairway. Reversa swept back into the dungeon, a smug grin lighting her face. "Thank you for the information about the lubtassium," she said. "I was able to animate the stone soldiers! Now I have an army *and* a castle. It's perfect." She clutched the Thingumybob, running her hands over its surface. "And now, you will tell me how this little device works."

"It's kind of complicated..." Shmedley began, stalling.

"I think I can handle it," Reversa interrupted.

Shmedley fidgeted. "Well, it relies a bit on Easy Magic, alpha waves, and, um, intention..."

Reversa's eyes narrowed. "You will give me lessons on how to make it work."

Shmedley hesitated. "Okay," he said meekly.

"No, Shmedley!" Boss cried. "You cannot! Teaching Reversa how to use the Thingumybob would be disastrous!"

Reversa blinked. "*Reversa*, eh? Interesting name. I like it. Yes, you can call me *Reversa*." She smiled sweetly at them. "How about this: I'll just leave you two down here, without food, for a few days. We'll see how that changes your minds about helping me. And if that doesn't work... we'll see what information my stone soldiers can drag out of you."

With that, she turned and left the dungeon.

"Oh, Boss, what are we going to do?" asked Shmedley.

"I... I don't know," said Boss sadly, bowing his head. "I don't know what we CAN do."

A little while later, Boss fell asleep. Shmedley stayed awake, staring into the darkness. Suddenly, he heard quiet footsteps coming down the dungeon stairs. He stood up and peered through the bars, half-expecting to see Reversa again.

Instead, he saw Doggie tiptoeing towards them.

"Doggie!" he cried.

"Hi," said Doggie. "I came back after you guys. And I stole *this* from that lady." He held out the Thingumybob.

"You're a genius!" cried Shmedley.

Boss woke up. He blinked through the bars at Doggie. "Mr. Munchabunch! I must insist that you stay—"

Then he saw that Doggie was holding the Thingumybob.

"Oh! Well! Actually, you've been quite useful on this journey. I think you've more than proven yourself."

A furious scream echoed down from somewhere above, making the walls of the dungeon shiver.

"Oh no," Shmedley whispered, eyes wide. "I think Reversa's figured out you've taken the Thingumybob."

"Uh oh," Doggie muttered. He hurried to pass the Thingumybob through the cell bars, but it was too thick to fit.

"*You're* going to have to use it, Mr. Munchabunch," Boss said.

Just then, Reversa came flying down the stone stairs, her eyes blazing with fury. She halted when she saw Doggie, momentarily thrown off. "Another talking beast?" she snarled, her gaze narrowing.

Then she spotted the Thingumybob clutched in Doggie's paws, and for the briefest moment, fear flashed across her face.

"Don't worry, Mr. Munchabunch," Boss called out encouragingly. "We'll teach you how to use it!"

Reversa's eyes widened, then she broke into a cruel smile. "Oh, he doesn't know how to use it yet? Perfect."

"Oh dear me," Boss muttered, looking flustered. "I shouldn't have said that."

"No, Boss," Shmedley agreed.

Reversa advanced toward Doggie, her hands already glowing with dark, crackling energy.

Shmedley shouted through the bars, "Doggie! Just use your feelings and press some random buttons!"

"Oh!" Doggie yelped, aiming the Thingumybob and pressing a couple of buttons at random. A pulse of lavender light shot out and struck Reversa, turning her hair a vivid shade of purple.

"Oh, very funny," Reversa sneered.

Doggie frantically pressed another button, and suddenly Reversa began to swell, inflating like a balloon. Her belly grew comically large, and she wobbled precariously, glaring at them.

"You will stop this *immediately!*" she roared, raising her hands to unleash a torrent of Dark Magic.

"Quick! Press the turquoise and magenta buttons at the same time!" Shmedley yelled. "And toggle the intention switch 17° to the left!"

"Ahh!" Doggie shouted, mashing a flurry of random buttons in a panic. A beam of light fired from the Thingumybob, hitting Reversa just as she was about to unleash her spell. She shrank back to her normal size but was now encased in a strange, translucent bubble. The bubble glowed with a soft blue aura, freezing her in place. She could blink, but her body was otherwise motionless.

"Excellent work!" Shmedley said, beaming. "You've trapped her in a time bubble. We're safe... for the moment."

"Yes, but the keys to our cell are in *her* pocket, and *she's* inside the bubble!" Boss pointed out.

Doggie's ears perked up, and he reached into his pocket with a grin. "Oh—I also took the keys from her while she was sleeping!"

Boss blinked in astonishment. "Mr. Munchabunch, you truly are a wonder!"

Doggie unlocked the cell, and the three of them slipped past Reversa, who glared at them helplessly from within her bubble.

They raced up the dungeon stairs, their footsteps echoing in the eerie silence.

"We've got a few minutes until that bubble bursts," Shmedley said, glancing nervously over his shoulder.

"Okay," Doggie replied.

They sprinted through the castle, making for the front door, only to find a group of stone soldiers standing guard. One of the soldiers tilted its head, its voice echoing dully. "Intruders? We kills you?"

"Uh, no," Doggie said quickly, thinking on his feet. "We're friends of your master. That's why we're already *inside* her castle. We're not intruders... so, you don't need to stop us!"

The soldiers looked at each other, then stepped aside. "Oh," one said. "Okay."

Doggie, Boss, and Shmedley dashed past, escaping into the wetland forests. Behind them, they heard Reversa's furious scream as she broke free from the bubble.

"Oh no," Shmedley gasped. "We've got to go! Quick, quick, quick!"

They scrambled to the *Paradox* and clambered aboard. Boss and Shmedley furiously pressed buttons, and the ship roared to life. In a blink, they were gone, whisked away into the timestream and onto their next adventure.

The Wild Beasts of Nerak

"ALL RIGHT," SAID BOSS. "Our next mission is to the unexplored country of Nerak, in western Magic Woods. No Meemie or Stick Person has ever returned from that land."

"Why not?" asked Doggie. "Is it dangerous?"

"Well, that's what we aim to find out. Now, let us go."

"Can I please be allowed out of the vehicle this time?" asked Doggie.

"Yeah, Boss," said Shmedley. "Why can't he come out with us? He's proven himself."

"It should be fine for him to accompany us," said Boss. "Well, unless it's *too* dangerous."

"That doesn't sound very reassuring," mumbled Doggie.

"We're going to the past, before the Changing of the World, when Nerak was still connected to Magic Woods," said Boss. "At the far western end of Nerak is supposed to be a World Tree, an oak named *Tensu*."

"What's a World Tree?" asked Doggie.

"Well, they are giant trees," answered Boss. "One at each corner of the world. They reach up to the Forest in the Sky, if the old stories can be believed."

"What's the Forest in the Sky?" asked Doggie.

Boss frowned. "I don't... well, *nobody* really knows for sure. It's supposed to be a world of everlasting peace and happiness, according to some."

"Ooh!" said Doggie. "Can we go there next?"

"No," said Boss. "No one can get up there."

"Well, we've never *tried*," said Shmedley.

"Yes, we've never tried," agreed Boss. "Because if we did, I'm sure we would be destroyed. The Forest in the Sky does not allow visitors. Now, come. Let's see what Nerak looked like, some 3000 years in the past."

They burst out of the timestream, the *Paradox* soaring over an arid, savanna-like landscape. Below, tall yellow grasses stretched as far as the eye could see, punctuated by clusters of gnarled brown trees. The land teemed with enormous prehistoric mammals: saber-toothed cats prowled near rocky outcrops, brontotheriums lumbered in herds, mastodons ambled by the watering holes, and the towering shapes of baluchitheriums moved like living mountains across the plains.

"Wow, Boss," Shmedley breathed, eyes wide with wonder.

"What are those *monsters*?" Doggie asked, his voice tinged with awe (and a touch of fear).

Boss adjusted his spectacles, peering down at the colossal creatures. "These, Mr. Munchabunch, are prehistoric mammals."

"They're *huge!*" Doggie exclaimed.

"Yes, they are," Boss agreed. "Let's land the ship and take a closer look."

They brought the *Paradox* down near the edge of a large lake. "This must be Lake Kitra," said Boss as they stepped cautiously out of the timeship, their feet sinking into the soft mud.

Shmedley's ears perked up as he listened to the cacophony of prehistoric life. The air buzzed with sounds: deep, rumbling calls from animals at the water's edge, strange hoots and hollers echoing across the plains, and, most delightfully to Shmedley's ears, the songs of unfamiliar birds. "Boss!" he said, eyes lighting up with excitement. "I hear so many bird species I've never heard before! And—if I'm not mistaken—a beige bunting!"

Boss stifled a yawn. "That's... very interesting, Shmedley."

"*I* think it's interesting," said Doggie.

Boss surveyed the landscape. "This place doesn't seem *that* dangerous," he remarked. "If you're small and quick, it should be easy to avoid the larger mammals."

Doggie frowned. "Then why does no one ever come back from here?"

Shmedley's ears twitched. "Uh oh," he said, his voice suddenly tense. "I think something's moving in the tall grass."

Boss and Doggie listened, straining to hear. The golden grass swayed gently in the wind, and for a moment, everything seemed still.

"Probably nothing," Boss said, though his voice wavered. "But we should stay alert—"

Suddenly, a massive snake shot out of the underbrush, lunging straight for Doggie.

"Ahhh!" Doggie screamed, scrambling backward.

Shmedley sprang into action, zapping the serpent with the Thingumybob. The gigantic snake's eyes went blank. It slithered away, confused, disappearing back into the grass.

Boss adjusted his bowtie. "Well, perhaps this land is full of predators lurking in the grass, ready to eat anything that dares to wander through."

Their conversation was cut short by a deep rumbling that shook the ground beneath their feet. "What's that?" Doggie asked.

Shmedley frowned. "Is it an earthquake, Boss?"

"No," said Boss. "I believe it's a herd of very large somethings heading our way. Shmedley, get a look!"

Shmedley scampered up one of the long blades of grass, shielding his eyes from the harsh sunlight. His heart sank as he spotted a thundering herd of brontotheriums charging straight toward them. "We're gonna get trampled!" he cried, jumping down and landing hard on the ground. Doggie hurried to help him up.

"Quick!" Boss shouted. "Into the *Paradox*!"

They bolted for the timeship, lifting off the ground just as the herd thundered past. One of the enormous brontotheriums swung its massive horn, smacking the *Paradox* and sending it spinning out of control.

"Whoa!" Doggie and Shmedley yelled as they tumbled around the cockpit, clinging to anything they could grab.

Boss lunged for the controls, wrestling the ship back into stability. "Let's gain some altitude," he said breathlessly. "Out of the range of those beasts."

The *Paradox* rose higher, and they watched the herd stampede below, kicking up clouds of dust. Doggie pressed his paws to the window. "It's like all the animals in this land don't want us here," he said.

"Interesting theory," said Boss, stroking his chin. "Maybe this land protects itself from outsiders. The beasts here are like antibodies, destroying invaders from without."

"That would certainly explain why no one's ever returned from this land," said Shmedley.

"Do you think WE'RE ever gonna return from this land?" asked Doggie.

"I hope so," said Boss.

Shmedley twisted his hands nervously. "Boss? While we're here, maybe we could visit Tensu? Because no one's ever seen that tree, as far as we know."

Boss frowned. "Well, seeing Tensu is not really that important *scientifically*..."

"But there might be unusual new bird species out there, on the World Tree," said Shmedley.

"Come on," said Doggie, looking at Boss. "We're *here*, in Nerak. We might as well go see Tensu."

Boss sighed. "All right. It *would* be good to confirm that there IS a World Tree there, I suppose. But let's activate the cloaking mechanism, so no flying creatures see us and try to stop us on the way."

He pressed the cloaking button, so the machine turned invisible. Then they headed west. As they flew over the wide fields of Nerak, Doggie looked out the window at the herds of prehistoric animals down below. Most were mammals, but there were a couple of dinosaurs as well... including a triceratops and a monoclonius. The dinosaurs looked ancient, the last survivors of their kind.

At last they approached Tensu, the World Tree at the Western Edge of the World. It was a gigantic oak that reached all the way up to the sky. They couldn't even see the top, for it was lost in the clouds.

They landed the *Paradox* and stepped outside. They saw a gigantic prehistoric sloth on the north side of the tree, standing on its back legs and licking the lowest branches with a derpy expression on its face.

"What's *that* thing?" asked Doggie.

Boss was about to answer, when all of a sudden the beast itself spoke. "I am a megatherium," it said, in a deep, slow voice. "A prehistoric sloth."

"Nice to meet you, Mr. Megatherium!" said Doggie.

"My name is Trope," said the giant sloth.

"Oh. Nice to meet you, Trope!"

Boss stood as tall as he could (although he was still only about the size of one of the megatherium's claws). "My name is Boston Ignatius Fuddlebluster, and this is my assistant, Shmedley."

Shmedley smiled. "And this is our *new* assistant, Doggie Cornelius Munchabunch."

"He's not *officially* an assistant yet," said Boss.

"How do you do?" said Trope, and then he went back to licking leaves again.

"So, Mr. Trope," said Boss. "I notice you are the only animal out here, by the Tree."

"That's right," said Trope.

"Are you the only animal in Nerak who can talk?"

Trope stopped licking. A sad expression passed over his face. "There used to be another one. My wife, Cliché. She used to lick the leaves on the south side of the tree. But now she is dead. And soon old Trope will be gone, too. I am very ancient."

"I'm so sorry," said Doggie, feeling heartsick at the thought of losing a loved one.

"Trope and Cliché were here when Tensu was just an acorn," said the old megatherium. "They were here when the first raindrops fell."

"Indeed?" said Boss. "Sounds like you've been here a long time. Can you tell us... has anyone else ever seen this World Tree?"

"And are there any unique bird species here?" asked Shmedley.

"Lots of animals have seen this tree," said Trope between licks. "Lots of birds, too."

"Well, what about anyone who can *talk*?" asked Boss. "Like Stick People, or Meemies?"

"There were two," said Trope. "Two only. A Stick Person, and a Meemie with black wings. They came here many years ago. They came on a boat that sailed over the snow."

"A boat that sailed over the snow?" said Doggie.

Trope nodded. "It was a long winter. And they made a fast boat that sailed across the snow, and that's how they crossed Nerak without getting attacked."

"Interesting," said Boss. "So, we're *not* the first outsiders to see this World Tree."

"No," said Trope, still licking. "But you will probably be the last."

"That's kind of creepy," Doggie muttered.

Suddenly they could hear a buzzing sound coming from inside the *Paradox*. Boss winced. "I fear we may have suffered some damage when that brontotherium whacked us," he said. "We need to inspect the machine, Shmedley."

"Sure thing, Boss," said Shmedley resignedly.

"I can help!" said Doggie.

"I think it might be better, Mr. Munchabunch, if you stayed out here," said Boss. "But don't travel too far. And don't fall off the Edge of the World."

"Okay!" said Doggie, scampering away with reckless abandon.

The Grace of Good Luck

BOSS AND SHMEDLEY WENT back into the *Paradox*. Doggie explored the area near the base of the tree, sniffing around. He found a big gray rock that was perfectly oval.

Old Trope said, "That is the last egg of the meat-eating brontosaurus rexes that once roamed this land."

"What's a meat-eating brontosaurus rex?" asked Doggie.

"They were a kind of long-necked dinosaur that could suck up animals and objects larger than themselves. But they are all extinct now, and that is the last egg."

Doggie looked at the egg. "I feel bad for the little fellow inside here."

"I'm sure that egg is dead by now," said Trope. "Don't you?"

"I guess so," said Doggie. "It DOES look a little fossilized."

The sun began to set, sinking into the misty unknown of the *Really* Weird Lands to the west. Doggie marveled at the beauty as the last rays of sunlight pierced through the dense branches of the tree.

Eager for a better view, Doggie clambered up the trunk of the massive tree, settling himself on one of its thick branches. From his perch, the sunset was even more breathtaking. The warm light bathed him in a gentle glow. He noticed tiny glowing golden puffs drifting lazily through the air. They seemed to be made of sunbeam dust, shimmering as they coated the branches and floated like delicate specks of pollen. Curious, Doggie reached out and carefully picked up one of the glowing puffs, examining it in wonder.

A soft, melodic voice broke the quiet. "I didn't know dogs could climb trees."

Startled, Doggie turned to see a small woman perched gracefully on a nearby branch. She looked almost human, but not quite. She had delicate wings, like a fairy, and she seemed to radiate an aura of gentle power. Her long golden hair shimmered with its own light, and specks of the glowing golden dust clung to it like tiny stars.

"Oh, hello there!" Doggie said, his voice a little shaky. "You startled me just a bit."

The woman's smile was kind. "I am Saffron Friday," she said. "The Grace of Good Luck."

"Nice to meet you!" Doggie replied. "My name is Doggie Cornelius Munchabunch."

"I know who you are," said Saffron Friday with a knowing smile.

"You do?" Doggie asked, his eyes widening.

"Indeed," she replied. "I know a great many things." As she spoke, more of the golden puffs drifted toward her, gathering in her glowing hair as if drawn by an invisible force.

Doggie watched them in awe. "What are those little golden things?" he asked.

"These are particles of bliss," Saffron Friday explained.

"What's bliss?" Doggie asked.

"Pure happiness and joy," she replied. "Bliss is created by the last light of the sun as it filters through these branches at sunset, on only one particular Friday each year. And you, my friend, are fortunate enough to be here on that day."

"Oh," Doggie said. "Well, that *is* lucky."

Saffron Friday laughed. "Indeed, it is. I gather this Bliss in my hair, and then I secretly pass by deserving mortals, showering them with the golden dust that I leave in my wake. That's where good luck comes from."

"Well, that's nice of you!" said Doggie.

The woman laughed again. "It is merely what I do."

Doggie couldn't help staring at her hair. "Your hair is so beautiful. It's like a special kind of yellow."

"It is saffron yellow," said Saffron Friday. "Technically, it's the color of the last rays of sunset on a Friday afternoon, shining through jars of purest honey that have been suffused with a goddess's golden tears."

"Oh," said Doggie.

"But you can just call it saffron yellow."

"Well, it's really lovely," said Doggie.

The sun finally dipped below the horizon, and the little yellow puffs of bliss faded away, vanishing with the last rays of daylight. But the golden particles in Saffron Friday's hair continued to glow, shining brightly in the deepening twilight.

Saffron Friday turned to leave. "It was nice to meet you, Doggie," she said. "Consider yourself lucky... not many mortals get to see a numen like me and live to tell the tale."

Doggie's eyes widened. "Oh," he said, blinking in surprise. "Well, I guess since *you're* lucky, that made *me* lucky too."

Saffron Friday laughed, a sound like silver bells chiming in the evening air. She floated upward, her wings catching a warm breeze. Just as she was about to take flight, she turned her head, and one of her radiant golden locks swished through the air, smacking Doggie right in the face. The impact released a cloud of bliss that showered over him, sparkling like tiny suns.

Saffron Friday glanced back, a sly smile curving her lips. "Whoops!" she said mischievously. "Sorry about that." Then, with a flick of her wings, she drifted into the sky, vanishing into the last traces of sunset.

The bliss soaked into Doggie, seeping all the way to his soul, where it became a part of him forever... though he had no idea. A warm, golden joy settled inside him.

He lingered on the branch a moment, then climbed down the tree and did a little more exploring at the base of the massive trunk while there was still a little light left. He found a stone with the word "Sellecca" carved into it.

Doggie looked up at Trope. "Mr. Trope? What does *Sellecca* mean?"

"It means *nightfall*, in the old tongue," said Trope, licking the leaves with HIS old tongue. "That was the name of the Meemie with the black wings, a warrior who fought for good. She is buried there."

"Oh," said Doggie. "What about the Stick Person who came with her?"

"She tried to return home on her snowboat," answered Trope. "I don't know what became of her after that. Old Trope doesn't know everything."

"Oh," said Doggie. He saw the fossilized egg and laid across it. "Poor thing," he said to himself. "The last of its kind. I wish it could have had better luck."

The egg began to move.

Doggie jumped off. "It's moving!" he said.

Cracks appeared in the side of the egg.

"It's hatching!" cried Doggie.

Trope stopped licking. He looked down, surprised. "It is," he said. "You should be careful."

Shmedley and Boss came out of the *Paradox* at that moment. "All right," said Boss. "We seem to have fixed the problem, Mr. Munchabunch."

Then they noticed the big egg beginning to hatch.

"Oh, what have you discovered there?" said Boss.

"Is it some sort of giant bird egg?" asked Shmedley, reaching for his journal.

"No," said Doggie. "I think it's a dinosaur."

The long neck of a little brontosaurus popped out of the egg. It made a small peeping noise.

"Oh, what a cutie!" said Doggie.

But then the dinosaur tried to suck Doggie up like it was a powerful vacuum cleaner. It caught Doggie by the tail and started sucking him into its tiny mouth.

"Help!" cried Doggie, already half-swallowed.

Shmedley and Boss rushed to help him, grabbing hold of Doggie's front paws and pulling with all their might. The dinosaur's suction power was strong, and for a moment, it seemed like they would lose Doggie to the beast's belly. But with one final, desperate tug, the salamanders managed to yank Doggie free. He popped out of the dinosaur's mouth with a loud *schlorp*, and the three of them tumbled backward, landing in a heap on the grass.

The brontosaurus seemed not to notice. He busied himself sucking up bits of broken eggshell, and then began eating leaves and bugs.

Doggie rubbed his midsection. "That thing almost sucked me up!"

"That is what those creatures do," said Trope. "They were a menace. Although, they WERE very effective at removing foreign invaders from this land."

Boss nodded. "Well, Mr. Munchabunch, let's go. You're lucky to be alive."

As they walked away, they heard the little brontosaurus cry out sadly.

Doggie looked back. "I feel bad for the little guy," he said.

"He'll be fine," said Boss.

"Actually, he *won't*," said Trope. "He will be killed by predators. The meat-eating brontosaurus rexes were not liked by the other animals. He might be able to suck up a few before they kill him, but he is too small to defend himself for long."

"Oh no!" said Doggie. "We can't just leave him here! He's the last of his kind!"

"Of course we can leave him," said Boss. "That's his fate. His destiny."

"But... maybe he could travel with us," said Doggie. "We can bring him somewhere safer."

"It sounds like he would suck things up wherever he goes," said Boss. "He'd be a menace."

"Well," said Doggie desperately, "couldn't you use the Thingumybob to make him a little smarter or something, so he can make better choices?"

Shmedley looked at Boss and shrugged. "It's possible."

"I don't think that's a good idea," said Boss.

But Shmedley was already adjusting dials and buttons on the Thingumybob. He blasted the little brontosaurus with green light, and then the dinosaur looked at them and said, "I'm hungry."

Trope stopped licking and looked down again, surprised.

"Hello," said Doggie, cautiously approaching the young brontosaurus. "My name's Doggie. What's *your* name?"

"I don't have a name," said the little brontosaurus.

"Hmm," said Doggie. "How about we call you.... Bliss?"

"Okay," said the brontosaurus. Then he hiccuped and said, "I'm hungry," again.

"Well, you're welcome to suck up things that you need to eat, like plants," said Doggie. "But don't suck up animals. And definitely not me!"

"Okay," said Bliss.

Doggie turned to Shmedley and Boss. "See? He's not a meat-eater anymore, and he won't suck anything up that he's not supposed to." He looked up at Trope. "So, the other animals don't have to worry anymore. Bliss is aware now. And he is only gonna eat plants."

"I'm afraid the other animals won't understand, or care," said Trope. "This little fellow is gonna be in trouble."

"Oh no!" said Doggie. He turned to his companions. "Please, Boss and Shmedley? We gotta bring him with us. He could be one of our companions!"

Boss shook his head. "Do you know how big those things get? No, it would be impossible for him to be our companion for long. Someday soon, he won't even fit inside the store room of the *Paradox*."

Doggie bowed his head.

Boss nodded at the little brontosaur and said, "I'm sorry, Mr. Bliss, but you will need to stay here, and manage as best you can."

"Okay," said the little dinosaur sadly.

At that moment, there was another crackling sound from inside the *Paradox*. A thin line of black smoke rose from one of the rear panels.

Boss whipped his head around. "Oh, goodness gracious me!" He and Shmedley rushed back into the ship, down into the engine room for more repairs.

Doggie looked at Bliss, and then he looked at the entryway to the *Paradox*. He thought, *I bet I could hide him inside the store room pretty easily...*

CHAPTER 8

Slow-Motion Liquid Fireworks

AT LAST, THE PARADOX was ready again. They took off into the timestream.

Shmedley went into the store room to grab a new pencil (he had dropped his old one somewhere in Nerak). He was very surprised, to say the least, to see Bliss the brontosaur standing there.

"Oh!" he said, jumping a little.

Doggie rushed into the room. "I didn't wanna leave him behind," he explained. "He would have gotten killed in Nerak!"

"I understand," said Shmedley. "But I don't think Boss is gonna like this."

Boss called to them from the cockpit. "Shmedley, Doggie, it is time for our next adventure!"

Doggie looked at Shmedley pleadingly. "Please don't say anything yet?"

"Okay," said Shmedley. "Let's just leave Bliss here for now."

"Thank you," said Doggie. He smiled at Bliss. "We'll get you some food soon."

Doggie's own tummy grumbled.

"YOU are gonna need some food soon!" said Shmedley.

"I know," said Doggie. "I *am* a little hungry. Wonder what my first food will be?"

Boss called to them again. "Shmedley! Doggie! Come!"

Doggie and Shmedley went to the cockpit of the *Paradox*, leaving Bliss behind in the storeroom.

"All right," said Boss. "Our next adventure will be to someplace you've always wanted to see, Shmedley."

Shmedley clapped his hands. "BirdSanktuary-land!?"

"No, no, a place of *historical* importance."

"Oh," said Shmedley, deflating.

"We're going to the moment when the Hollow Mountains first appeared!"

"Hollow Mountains?" said Doggie.

"Yes, my lovely hound. There are five of them. Although, most folk only know about four of them. You lived inside one, Mr. Munchabunch, for a brief moment... the mountain named *Yesterday's Macaroni.*"

Doggie's tummy growled again.

"Now," continued Boss, "these mountains appeared after The Pumpkin froze himself—and all those around him—in time. Something happened to the world that day. Our theory is that The Pumpkin inadvertently ripped a hole in time and space—or at least in the fabric of reality—that made a bunch of dreamstuff from the Weird Lands come into Magic Woods and create the Hollow Mountains."

"What are the Weird Lands?" asked Doggie.

"The weird misty realm that surrounds Magic Woods, whence come dreams."

"It was that weird nothingness past the World Tree," added Shmedley.

"Oh!" said Doggie. "And who, or what, is The Pumpkin?"

"A diabolical woodland jack-o'lantern," said Boss. "We are going back to the night that Versa brought him back to life, the very dawn of the Fourth Age."

"Or the very end of the *Third* Age, really," said Shmedley.

"Yes," agreed Boss. "Indeed, it is *when* The Pumpkin freezes himself in time that the Third Age ends and the Fourth Age begins. And we are going to that time, to see how the Hollow Mountains came to be."

"Which Hollow Mountain?" asked Shmedley.

"We're going right to the center of Magic Woods," answered Boss. "Right where Yesterday's Macaroni will appear.

"Sounds exciting," said Shmedley.

"It should be," said Boss. "Now, we're going back about four years—as measured in OUTSIDE time—before YOU appeared, Mr. Munchabunch."

Doggie shrugged. "Okay."

Boss opened a little drawer in the console and produced three biscuits. He handed one each to Doggie and Shmedley. "I've been saving these for a special occasion," he said.

"Are these from that bakery in Atisket in the Third Age?" asked Shmedley.

"Yes! And they shouldn't be *too* stale." Boss took a tentative nibble. "Yep... they're still good. Enjoy!"

Shmedley started nibbling on his biscuit.

Doggie looked at his biscuit and felt his tummy growl. But he wanted to make sure Bliss had enough to eat. "I'm gonna eat this in the store room," he said, exiting the cockpit.

"Suit yourself," said Boss. "But don't get crumbs everywhere, my boy!"

"I won't!" Doggie promised.

He went into the storage room and he gave the biscuit to Bliss. "Thank you!" said the grateful dinosaur, and he sucked it up in a second.

"I wish I had *more* food for you," said Doggie. "I'll try to get you something else soon."

At last, the *Paradox* slipped gracefully out of the timestream, emerging into a world bathed in sunlight. They soared over a field bursting with wildflowers.

"Look at all those colors!" said Doggie, peering out the window.

They brought the *Paradox* to a gentle stop. They stepped out of the ship and took a look around. The air was filled with the hum of bees and the songs of birds.

"What a wonderful flowery field!" Doggie exclaimed, his nose twitching with delight.

"Yes," said Boss. "So, this is Flowerfield, as you can see. And this is where, sometime tonight, Yesterday's Macaroni will appear. In fact, tonight is the night when ALL the Hollow Mountains will appear... and we'll be right here, in the center of the world, able to see the whole thing! Front row seats!"

Doggie's stomach let out a loud, rumbling growl. Meanwhile, Shmedley and Boss were plucking bugs from the grass and eating them. Shmedley held up a plump beetle, offering it to Doggie. "Want some?" he asked.

Doggie wrinkled his nose. "I'd rather not have *bugs* as my first taste of food, but thanks anyway!" He paused, a thoughtful frown forming on his face. "Wait a second... didn't you say we couldn't even *step* on a butterfly because it could change the future? Why are you eating bugs?"

Boss crunched down on a cricket, swallowing with a satisfied sigh. "Ah, yes," he said. "That was when we were thousands of years in the past. But right now, we're only about fifty years away from the end of this world. The odds of causing a major shift in the timeline by munching on a few bugs here and now are quite slim."

"Oh," said Doggie.

Boss wiped his mouth with his handkerchief. "Well, we might as well make ourselves at home for a bit." He yawned loudly. "Actually, I think I might even take a little nap. We have a few hours until nightfall, when the mountains appear."

"Okay, Boss," said Shmedley.

Boss walked back into the *Paradox* and curled up on his little bed in the sleeping quarters.

Doggie looked at Shmedley. "I think I'll take Bliss outside," he said.

"Okay," said Shmedley. "But I'd wait until Boss is sleeping. Shouldn't take *too* long... he loves napping."

Doggie waited a few minutes, then snuck into the *Paradox*. He tiptoed past the sleeping quarters (where he could hear Boss snoring softly) and opened the door to the storeroom. "Wanna come outside?" he whispered to the hungry brontosaur.

"Okay," said Bliss.

"You just have to walk quietly."

"Okay," said Bliss. Then he added, "I'm hungry."

"Don't worry," said Doggie. "There's a whole world outside, full of plants you can eat."

"Yum," said Bliss.

They snuck outside, and the brontosaurus started sucking up flowers and bugs and grass. "It's all so tasty!" he said.

"Good!" said Doggie.

When evening came, Boss stepped out of the *Paradox* and stretched his arms. "Ohhh, that was a nice little nap," he said, scanning the field. Suddenly he noticed Bliss, munching on a patch of dandelions.

"Wait a minute," he said. "Where did HE come from? I didn't know that meat-eating brontosaurus rexes lived *here*, in Flowerfield! Shmedley, mark this information down!"

"Actually," said Doggie, "It's Bliss, from Nerak. I snuck him on board the *Paradox*."

Boss frowned deeply. "That's... well, that's not acceptable." He called to the brontosaur, who was busy grazing. "Mr. Bliss, I'm afraid we'll have to bring you back to Nerak."

"His name is *Bliss*," said Doggie. "Not MISTER Bliss. He's not a grownup yet."

"Well, someday soon he *will* be," said Boss. "This species grows fast, you know."

"But he would have been killed back in his land!" Doggie cried. "We can't take him back!"

Boss sighed. "Well, we'll figure out what to do later. Right now, we should get ready for the show." He stood tall and cleared his throat. "Picture it, if you will... at this very moment, several hopkins to the west, in the city of Atisket—well, actually, just *outside* the city of Atisket—Versa is about to call you-know-who back to life."

"Good thing you didn't say his name," said Shmedley.

"Yes," agreed Boss. "Then *I* would have called him back to life."

"Who?" asked Doggie.

"Never you mind," said Boss. "We can't say his name, or he'll come back to life HERE instead of there."

"He's a big round evil orange thing full of seeds," said Shmedley, winking.

"Ah," said Doggie. "Got it."

"He ends up freezing himself and everyone around him in time tonight, but we don't know precisely *when* that happens. All we know is that, when he splits Magic Woods into two timeworlds, the Hollow Mountains appear."

"We *think*," added Shmedley.

"Yes, we *think*," said Boss. "So, everyone, watch the skies carefully!"

"Why the skies?" asked Doggie.

"I don't really know," said Boss, frowning. "I just have a feeling that's where the magic will come from."

"Sounds good to me!" said Doggie.

Shmedley took out a blanket and spread it on the grass. They all lay on their backs and looked up at the sky. They could hear Bliss contentedly munching dandelions all around them. "*You* should try a dandelion," said Bliss to Doggie. "They taste kinda like ear wax."

"Um, no thanks," said Doggie, shuddering. "I'm not THAT hungry yet. And besides, I want my first food to be something delicious."

They laid on the blanket a long time, but nothing happened. "This is strange," said Boss. "I didn't think it would have taken *this* long for Versa to call you-know-who back to life."

"Maybe we messed with the timeline again," said Shmedley.

Doggie's ears perked up as he caught the sound of that distant, eerie voice echoing through the air. *"Who's the Special Boo?"*

Doggie turned to Boss and Shmedley. "Oh yeah," he said. "I've been meaning to ask... who's the Special Boo?"

The salamanders flinched as if they'd been struck by lightning. Boss spun around, his eyes wide with alarm. "Why are you asking us that?" he demanded, his voice trembling with fear.

"Uh, because I keep hearing a voice asking, *'Who's the Special Boo?'* And I was just wondering what it meant."

"Oh dear," Shmedley murmured, visibly shaking.

"Oh no no no," Boss muttered. *"The Special Boo.* That's what we call *him.*"

"Even though," Shmedley added, "he seems to be asking *for* the Special Boo. It's... confusing."

"Who *is* he?" Doggie asked, his curiosity now mixed with a growing sense of unease.

Boss swallowed hard. "He's... well, he guards the timeline," he explained. "And he comes after us when we've, um, meddled with history too much. By accident, of course."

Doggie's eyes widened. "What does he want?"

Boss fiddled nervously with his pocket watch. "Legend says that his voice gets louder the closer he gets to you."

"Makes sense," said Doggie.

"And when his voice becomes so loud that you can finally *see* him," Boss continued, his face grim, "it's already too late. He'll devour you—completely and utterly—all in the name of protecting the timeline, of course."

"That's *terrifying*!" Doggie exclaimed.

"I know," Shmedley agreed, still shivering from head to tail. "I know."

"Well, you gotta admire his dedication, though," said Boss. "He's just doing what he's supposed to do." He glanced over at Bliss, who was eating some wildflowers. "Maybe the Special Boo's getting closer because you rescued that brontosaurus rex and brought him to this time."

"I'm sorry," said Doggie.

All of a sudden Shmedley said, "Look!"

Doggie and Boss turned to look up at the sky. It was rippling and turning in on itself, in a wash of colors that looked like a nebula from beyond time and space.

"Gorgeous!" whispered Boss in awe. "This must be it! This must be the moment when The Pumpkin split time. That action allowed some of the Weird Lands to break through into Magic Woods."

The brightly colored weirdness rained down upon different parts of Magic Woods, looking like slow-motion liquid fireworks.

"It's pretty!" said Shmedley.

"It's pretty AND it's kind of scary!" said Doggie.

Even Bliss stopped eating long enough to look up, too.

Boss smiled wide, unable to hide his enthusiasm. "This is incredible! And we're right here, watching it."

A wash of the rainbow colored weirdness rippled through a fold in the night sky directly overhead, and then came straight down towards them.

"Uh," said Doggie. "I think it's heading straight for us!"

"Yes," said Boss dreamily. "I think it's about to create Yesterday's Macaroni..."

Shmedley sat up. "Boss, aren't we right on the spot where Yesterday's Macaroni will be?"

Boss frowned. Then he sat up and looked around. "Oh, dear me..."

Before they could get out of the way, the wash of liquid light rained down all around them. The predominant color was a rich yellow, the color of day-old macaroni and cheese.

"Oh no," said Doggie.

They felt themselves wrapped in a swirl of magic. And then, the next thing they knew, they were surrounded by complete blackness.

CHAPTER 9

Return of the Toad Instigators

THEY STOOD QUIETLY IN the blackness for a long moment, until at last Shmedley spoke. "Are we dead, Boss?"

"I don't think so," Boss answered. "I can feel my feet, and my tail. Plus, we're able to think and talk."

Shmedley called out into the darkness. "Are you here, Doggie?"

Doggie reached out with his paw until he found Shmedley's hand. "Yes, I'm here."

"Good."

Doggie called to Bliss. "Are YOU here, Bliss?"

They heard a voice, a little ways off. "Yep."

"Okay," said Boss. "So, we seem to be in some sort of *place*... hmm. The ground feels hard, like stone or tightly-packed dirt."

"I also feel something soft, like moss," said Shmedley.

"I wish there was light here," said Doggie.

All of a sudden, a strange light began to shine around them, a grayish glow, very dim. But it was bright enough for them to see that they were in some sort of subterranean jungle world full of wild plants.

"Look at this light," said Boss, astonished. "Where does it come from? It's incredible. We must be beneath Yesterday's Macaroni, in some sort of subterranean jungle world."

"Oh!" cried Bliss happily. "Look at all this food!" He started snacking on all different kinds of fruit. The fruit LOOKED like tomatoes, pineapples, and peaches. "These are delicious!" he said. He seemed to actually grow a little bigger as he ate. "This place is full of yummies!"

Shmedley turned to Doggie. "Maybe you should eat some of those."

"Ooh!" said Doggie. "Good idea." He approached a giant pineapple and sniffed it. "Mm. I like the smell of this one."

"I wouldn't eat that if I were you, Mr. Munchabunch," said Boss. "These subterranean fruits might be dangerous."

"But Bliss is eating them!"

"Well, brontosaurus rexes have unusual stomachs. They can eat anything. But that doesn't mean YOU can."

"All right," said Doggie sadly, pushing the pineapple aside and trying to ignore the hunger pangs in his belly.

Boss turned to Shmedley. "Do you have the Thingumybob handy?"

"Always, Boss."

"Good. You and I are going to explore a little bit, see if we can find a way out of this place." He turned back to Doggie. "You and Mr. Bliss stay here and watch the *Paradox*. Guard it as best you can."

"I don't know if I'd make a very effective guard," said Doggie. "It's not like I know karate or anything."

"You'll do fine," said Boss. "We just want to have a look around."

Boss and Shmedley wandered through the lush, otherworldly expanse of the subterranean jungle, weaving between towering ferns and vines that twisted up the rocky cavern walls. Bioluminescent flowers glowed gently in the dimness, casting an eerie, greenish light.

"It's incredible," Boss said, his eyes wide with wonder as they meandered deeper into the jungle. "How can plants grow down here without sunlight? It defies science!"

Shmedley glanced around, marveling at the towering plants. "How did they get here and grow so tall, Boss? Didn't this mountain only form a few minutes ago?"

"Yes," Boss replied. "But that's the beauty of these Hollow Mountains. The moment they come into existence, they're already ancient, backfilled with their own rich history and secrets."

"Oh, right," said Shmedley. "I knew that."

They pressed on, exploring several caverns and caves, each one brimming with dense jungle growth. After a while, Shmedley said, "Uh, Boss, do you remember the way back?"

"Of course I do, Shmedley!" Boss declared, though his eyes darted around uncertainly. "It's, uh... let's see..." He paused, turning in a slow circle. "Well, everything *does* look rather similar down here, doesn't it?"

"It does, Boss," Shmedley agreed.

"Yes. Hard to tell one cave from another," Boss admitted. "All right, let's try that left-hand cave over there. I have a feeling it'll loop us back around to the *Paradox*."

Shmedley frowned. "I think we should try to retrace our steps. You know, go back the way we came."

"No," Boss insisted confidently. "We're *more* likely to get lost that way. Let's press forward. See how this cave slopes to the right? It might just take us back."

"Okay," Shmedley said doubtfully. "You're the boss, Boss."

They kept walking, but with each step, the jungle seemed denser, the air heavier, and the path more unfamiliar. Eventually, Shmedley stopped in his tracks. "Boss," he said, "I really think we're lost."

Boss sighed. "Yes, Shmedley," he admitted. "It appears we are..."

All of a sudden, they felt a rumbling beneath their feet.

"Is it an earthquake?" said Shmedley.

"No," said Boss, his voice shaking from the growing rumble. "I believe the floor is about to erupt..."

All at once, thousands of wild toads erupted from the cavern floor, leaping and croaking in a chaotic frenzy. "Ahh!" Shmedley and Boss yelled, scrambling as the ground beneath them transformed into a surging mass of slippery, hopping toads. The writhing mound of amphibians lifted them higher and higher, rising like an unstoppable mountain.

"We're going to crash into the ceiling!" Shmedley shouted, eyes wide with panic.

Boss clung desperately to his hat. "Hold on to your hat, Shmedley!" he bellowed.

"I don't have one!" Shmedley yelped, flailing his arms as the toads kept pouring out of the cavern floor, carrying them ever upward. The rocky ceiling loomed dangerously close. They were seconds away from being squished against it.

"Use the Thingumybob!" Boss cried. "Make a hole!"

Shmedley fumbled for the Thingumybob. He aimed it shakily at the ceiling and twisted several knobs before slamming a button. A burst of brilliant silver light shot out, blasting a hole in the ceiling with a deafening *crack*.

"Get ready, Shmedley!" Boss shouted, bracing himself.

The toad wave erupted through the hole, spilling out onto the bustling streets of Yesterday's Macaroni. Startled animals shrieked, "Ah! We're being invaded! Look out, everybody!" Animals fled in terror, dashing into their homes.

Boss and Shmedley clung desperately to the churning mass of toads, trying to stay on top so they wouldn't be crushed. But the toad wave surged and bucked beneath them, making it increasingly difficult to keep their balance.

"I'm not very good at toad-surfing, Boss!" said Shmedley, flailing about.

"Quick!" Boss shouted, pointing frantically. "Into that big municipal building over there!"

They leaped off the wave of toads and dashed for the entrance of a large, stately building. They threw themselves through the doors and slammed them shut. The sounds of croaking and chaos echoed outside.

They soon realized they were not alone in there.

They turned and saw a hippo with three belly buttons, a crimson bear and a crimson ape, and a pinkish constrictor snake with two strange white things on either side of his face.

"The Youth Brigade!" said Shmedley.

"Who the heck are *you* guys?" snarled Mr. Constrictor.

The hippo said, "I saw them come out of the ground with the toads! They are the ones who let those beasts out!"

"Why did you do that to us?" asked Love Bear.

"Well, it's not really our fault," said Boss. "It was a coincidence. We just happened to be here on a Toad Day."

"A Toad Day?" said Love Ape skeptically.

"Yes. Twice a month or so this happens here. Yes?"

"It's never happened *before*," growled Mr. Constrictor.

"Oh," said Boss. "I guess we're here for the first."

"It'll stop eventually," said Shmedley. "I think the toad eruptions are connected to the lunar cycle."

"We're gonna connect YOU to a lunar cycle," said Mr. Constrictor, rising up like a cobra.

Boss whispered to Shmedley. "We gotta get out of here..."

"Agreed," said Shmedley.

"Run!" Boss shouted, and they bolted out the door, barely dodging a swipe from Mr. Constrictor's tail.

"And don't you *ever* come back!" Mr. Constrictor roared after them.

Boss and Shmedley raced headlong into a writhing wall of toads, which surged forward and nearly bowled them over. The sheer mass of slippery amphibians knocked Boss's hat clean off his head. "We're going to get squashed!" Boss cried, snatching up his hat and clutching it protectively. "Use the Thingumybob, Shmedley!"

Shmedley fumbled with the strange device, managing to freeze a few of the amphibians in place, but the tide of toads was relentless.

"We'll have to carve out a path," said Boss. "Freeze a few at a time and keep moving! Go, go, go!"

With a determined nod, Shmedley worked the Thingumybob, stunning toads one cluster at a time. They made slow but steady progress, scrambling through the squirming horde toward the front door of Yesterday's Macaroni. They flung it open and tumbled outside, landing in a heap. A few determined toads hopped after them, but most stayed inside the mountain, seemingly content with their new habitat.

"We made it!" Boss panted, dusting off his hat with a triumphant flourish.

Shmedley sat up, frowning deeply. "But poor Doggie's still inside," he said.

Boss's smile faded. "Yes," he sighed. "I'm afraid I have no idea how we're going to reach the *Paradox*. Maybe, if we wait for the toads to calm down, we can sneak back into the mountain..."

A sudden whirring noise filled the air, and they both looked up. To their astonishment, the *Paradox* was descending from the sky, wobbling slightly as it landed with a heavy thud nearby.

"What in the world is happening!?" Boss sputtered, his eyes wide with disbelief. "Who could possibly be piloting that thing?"

The ramp lowered, and out stepped Doggie, wagging his tail and beaming. "Hello!" he called cheerfully.

"Mr. Munchabunch!" Boss exclaimed, stunned. "How did you manage that? The landing was clumsy and amateurish, but remarkably good for a first attempt!"

"Thanks!" said Doggie. "Well, I've been watching you two pilot the *Paradox*, and I've picked up a few tricks. I just thought I'd give it a try! So I did a little temporal displacement, magnetic field-bending, spacetime-jump thing to get out of that cave under the mountain."

Boss's jaw dropped, and then he laughed, shaking his head in amazement. "Mr. Munchabunch, you're a genius!"

"Thanks!" Doggie said, grinning from ear to ear.

Shmedley frowned. "But where's Bliss?"

Doggie looked down sadly. "He was too big to fit on the ship. He's already grown too much. But he didn't really wanna come with me anyways... he said he wanted to STAY in that underground world and gorge himself on the plants down there. I bet he can survive down there for a long time."

"Indeed, he will," Boss murmured.

"Huh?" said Doggie.

"Nothing," said Boss. "Pretend I didn't say anything."

"All right..." said Doggie, puzzled.

"Well, Mr. Munchabunch, you are really proving yourself. But we'd better get out of here before the Town Elders look outside."

"Youth Brigade," said Shmedley.

"Right, the Youth Brigade."

"But I don't think they'll be able to get to us anytime soon," said Shmedley. "All those toads..."

"So true," said Boss. "But still..." He turned and headed for the *Paradox*. Shmedley and Doggie followed.

"Where are we going to next?" asked Doggie. "BirdSanktuary-land?"

"No, I'm afraid not," said Boss. "Our next mission is a very important one. We're going to find out what happened to Mr. Whisker Tomfoolery when he vanished from the historical record. We aim to find out whether he disappeared... or died."

CHAPTER 10

Mr. Tomfoolery

BOSS LEANED FORWARD, FINGERS flying over the *Paradox's* dashboard as he keyed in a series of coordinates. The console lit up with a soft hum. "All right," he said. "We know that Mr. Tomfoolery once tried to discover where the Elephants lived. He managed to sneak onto an Elephant Bus... and then, well, he was never seen again. But today, we're going to find out *exactly* what happened. We'll attach a bug to him, so we can hear everything he says."

"A bug?" said Doggie. "Like that stinkbug you squished?"

"No, not an actual *living* bug. A small recording device."

"Ah," said Doggie.

"With this device," Boss continued, "we'll be able to hear everything that transpires. It's like spying."

Doggie's eyes lit up. "Cool!"

"Indeed," said Boss. "All right, let's get ready."

The *Paradox* shuddered, its engines roaring to life, before rocketing forward and slicing through the timestream. For several minutes, they hurtled through a kaleidoscope of swirling colors and rippling light, time bending and warping around them. Then, with a gentle *thump*, the ship landed gracefully in a clump of tall grass just outside Crisscross Applesauce.

The door hissed open. Boss, Shmedley, and Doggie stepped out into the field. Boss looked through the binoculars, searching for Whisker.

"Look over there," Boss whispered, handing the binoculars to Doggie. A rat stood near the base of the mountain, whiskers twitching, with a mischievous glint in his eyes. He wore a small, bulging backpack, and he kept glancing around as if expecting to be followed.

"Is that Whiskers?" Doggie asked, passing the binoculars to Shmedley.

"Whisker," Boss corrected. "Yes, that's Mr. Tomfoolery, no doubt about it." He turned to Shmedley. "Shmedley, it's time. Place the bug."

"Got it," Shmedley whispered, crouching low. He moved quietly through the tall grass, making not a sound as he approached the unsuspecting Whisker. The mischievous rat stood there, oblivious, still fidgeting with his backpack and glancing around.

With delicate hands, Shmedley attached the tiny recording device to the back of Whisker's pack. The rat didn't even flinch.

Shmedley crept back the way he had come, slipping through the blades of grass.

"You're really good at being a sneaky spy!" said Doggie.

"Aw, thanks," said Shmedley.

All of a sudden, a huge yellow Elephant Bus appeared in the field. "What the heck is *that* thing?" cried Doggie. "A bus for elephants?"

"That's exactly what it is," said Boss. "Let's go into the *Paradox* so we can listen on the speakers."

They climbed into the cockpit. They could hear Whisker's voice coming through the speakers.

"Where are you headed?" he asked the Elephants.

"Jimmy's House," the Elephants replied.

"Aw, man," said Whisker. "That's not where I wanted to go. Oh well. Have a nice day."

Whisker pretended to walk away from the bus. But when the Elephants weren't looking, he jumped up and climbed through a slightly open window in the back.

"O-ho!" said Boss. "So *that's* how he sneaks on board."

"The Elephants aren't gonna be too happy if they see him," said Shmedley.

"True," said Boss. "But that *was* a good way for him to find out where the Elephants live. Presumably they stop at a home base at some point."

"I suppose so," said Shmedley.

Boss straightened his bowtie. "Well, let's cloak our ship, so it's invisible, and follow the bus. Luckily, there's a tracking device inside the bug we put on his backpack."

The Elephant Bus took off. The *Paradox* followed at a safe distance, through the strange vortex pathway tunnels that the Elephant Buses took through the Weird Lands.

Doggie looked out the window in wonder, gazing at all the misty dreamstuff passing by. "Whoa. What IS all this stuff we're zooming through right now?"

"The Weird Lands," said Shmedley. "It's where dreams take place."

"What's a dream?" asked Doggie.

"Oh, right," said Shmedley. "You haven't even *had* a dream yet."

Suddenly their speakers crackled, and they heard an Elephant say, "Hey! You can't be on our bus!"

They heard Whisker say, "Sorry... I got on by accident. Whoops!"

"You have to pay for the ride, or we'll throw YOU out the window!" said the Elephants.

"I got something alive in my backpack, I think," answered Whisker. "Lemme just look..."

Shmedley and Boss exchanged a meaningful glance.

"What's going on?" asked Doggie.

"Well, you're supposed to pay for each Elephant Bus ride by throwing something alive out the window," answered Boss. "A sacrifice for the Weird Lands, a living thing that will dissolve into dreamstuff."

The speaker crackled again. They heard Whisker say, "Ugh, sorry, I don't have anything alive in my backpack. But I can gladly pay you next Tuesday, if you give me the chance..."

"NO!" bellowed an Elephant. "No. *You* must be the sacrifice."

"Aaaack! No, please!"

Boss nodded. "So, that explains it. They throw him out the window. Mr. Tomfoolery didn't *disappear*... he died. He must have dissolved into dreamstuff."

Outside, Whisker was thrown from the Elephant Bus window. "Aaaaaahhhh!" He hurtled straight toward the *Paradox*.

"Shmedley, turn the ship!" Boss shouted, panic in his voice.

Shmedley scrambled at the controls, but it was too late. With a bone-rattling crash, Whisker smashed right through the front window, tumbling into the cockpit. A dozen red warning lights began flashing, and a deafening alarm blared through the ship.

Strange dreamstuff oozed into the cabin, twisting and curling through the air like living mist.

"Goodness gracious!" cried Boss. "This is a catastrophe! A disaster!"

"A *disastrophe*," said Doggie.

Whisker picked himself up, blinking dazedly. He rubbed his head. "What's going on?" he asked, staring around the damaged cockpit. Then he saw Doggie. "Doggie, what are you doing here?"

"Hi!" said Doggie. "How do you know my name?"

"I've known you for years, ya big galoot," said Whisker. He nodded at Boss and Shmedley. "What's the deal with these old-timey lizards?"

"We're *salamanders*," said Shmedley, offended.

"AND we're all about to die," said Boss, checking the gauges and instrument panels. The *Paradox* was twisting and turning wildly. "We're gonna have to make an emergency landing."

The *Paradox* crash-landed in the bushes outside Crisscross Applesauce. "We're back where we started," said Doggie. "When we were spying on Whisker."

"You were spying on me?" said Whisker.

"Yep!" said Doggie.

"Why?" asked Whisker. "And what in the name of tarnation is going on?" He looked at Boss and Shmedley. "Who ARE you guys? And why doesn't Doggie recognize me?"

"My name is Boston Ignatius Fuddlebluster, and this is my assistant, Shmedley."

Shmedley pointed to Doggie. "And this is our OTHER assistant, Doggie Cornelius Munchabunch the First."

Whisker blinked. "That's a *different* Doggie?"

"Yes, one from the past," said Boss.

"We're time travelers," said Shmedley.

"Whoa," said Whisker. He looked around the *Paradox* with renewed interest.

"Yes," said Boss. "We were trying to find out what happened when you vanished from the historical record."

"I vanish from the historical record?" said Whisker, trying to digest this news. "So, I disappeared?"

"Not exactly," answered Boss. "Actually, it turns out you were supposed to die."

"What!?"

"You got thrown into the Weird Lands, and must have dissolved into dreamstuff."

Whisker shook his head. "But I didn't dissolve! You guys saved me."

"Well," said Boss with a sigh. "We weren't supposed to."

Doggie heard a faint voice, faraway but clear. *"Who's the Special Boo?"*

"Well, thanks for saving me," said Whisker, heading for the door. "I'm heading back to my apartment in Crisscross Applesauce."

"You can't," said Boss, looking at a gauge. "You don't *have* your apartment yet."

"Huh?"

"It appears that, even though we returned to the site of our last stop, we arrived at a different point in time, about one year before you snuck on the Elephant Bus. When you were still in college."

"Wait," said Whisker. "I'm in the past right now? You mean, I could go inside the mountain and see myself?"

"Yes, Mr. Tomfoolery... and that would be a disaster! You could cause the very fabric of reality to unravel."

"Man!" said Whisker. "That's some pressure." He sighed. "Okay, just bring me back to my regular time."

"We can't," said Shmedley. "Our azidozide cells are completely depleted. The stress from the cockpit rupture must have drained them dry. We're stuck in this time period."

Boss sank into a chair with a heavy sigh, rubbing his temples. "Where in the world are we supposed to get azidozide now? It used to be mined in Penelopolee, ages ago—in the Third Age, back when Kay-Cee was the Red Queen. But we can't reach that time from here."

Whisker, who had been brushing bits of glass and dreamstuff from his fur, looked up thoughtfully. "I used to use azidozide for some of my experiments," he said. "I even kept a stash in my old laboratory."

"Yes," Boss said, "but that lab was in Yesterday's Macaroni, and we're a long way from there."

Whisker's eyes lit up. "Wait! When I went to college *here*, I had some azidozide in my workshop-slash-dorm room."

Boss sat bolt upright. "You mean... the evil version of you that's currently inside the mountain—"

"*Evil version?!*" Doggie said, taking a nervous step back.

Whisker sighed, looking a bit sheepish. "It's a long story..."

Boss leaned forward. "So, you're saying that the evil version of you, the one inside the mountain *right now*, should have some azidozide?"

Whisker nodded. "Yeah. He—or I—should have some."

Boss stood up, a spark of hope in his eyes. "Do you think we could break into your evil self's workshop and steal it? It's our only shot at getting back to the right time."

Whisker hesitated, then nodded slowly. "Sure, I think I can get us in. But I'll need help... someone to keep watch while I sneak in."

Boss considered this and then nodded. "We should be able to blend in pretty easily here in Crisscross Applesauce. It's a bustling town, full of animals who don't all know each other. We should be able to move through undetected and sneak our way to your workshop."

Whisker took a deep breath, adjusting his backpack straps. "All right," he said. "Let's do this."

The group gathered their gear and prepared to venture into the bustling city of Crisscross Applesauce, hoping not to get caught by Whisker's evil self.

☙ Chapter 11 ☙
Love Advice

THEY STROLLED UP TO the grand entrance of Crisscross Applesauce and stepped through the massive front doors.

"Whoa!" Doggie exclaimed, his eyes widening as he took in the bustling scene. "Look at all these animals! There must be hundreds of them, all different sorts and types!"

The college campus was alive with activity. Students of every imaginable species were singing songs, painting colorful murals, and engaging in lively, creative projects. The air was filled with music and laughter, and Doggie's tail began wagging furiously. "Oh, I think I wanna live here!" he said. "This place is amazing! Look at all the fun things to do!"

Boss scanned the crowd until his gaze landed on a shadowy figure. "There he is," he said, pointing to a suspicious-looking rat lurking by the entrance to a dark alleyway.

The good Whisker let out a low whistle. "Wow," he murmured, eyeing his doppelgänger. "I looked pretty sinister back then. But also kinda cool, tee hee hee!"

They watched as the evil Whisker cast a furtive glance around before slipping away into the shadows of the alley.

"Okay," the good Whisker said, his voice steady but tense. "I'm pretty sure that version of me is heading to a meeting of the Orange-Eye Club. This is our chance. While he's occupied, we should be able to sneak into my—or rather, *his*—lab. You three wait outside and keep watch for me."

Shmedley nodded. "As you wish," he said.

They made their way into the dormitory and quietly walked down the corridor until they reached Whisker's room. Shmedley,

Doggie, and Boss took up their positions beside the door. "This should only take a minute," Whisker whispered, disappearing into the room.

While they waited, Doggie's attention was drawn to a fancy rabbit strolling down the hall, singing a love song with an effortlessly smooth voice. *"In love all day and night you'll find me... with a gaggle of fans trailing right behind me..."* Sure enough, a group of adoring fans trailed after him, swooning and giggling with delight.

"Who's *that*?" Doggie asked, his eyes wide with awe.

"That," said Shmedley, "is Hare Pierre Meadowgrass, the world's greatest tenor."

Doggie's jaw dropped even further when Hare Pierre caught sight of him. The rabbit paused, a knowing smile on his face. "Hello, Doggie," he said.

Doggie blinked, astonished. "Oh, hello! You recognize me?"

"Of course," Hare Pierre laughed. "You and your bandmates are quite the competition. Not in the songwriting department, mind you, but certainly when it comes to sheer popularity. Your band has a *fairly* strong following."

"I'm in a band?" Doggie said, surprised.

Hare Pierre's smile was laced with pity. "You really aren't the brightest, are you?"

"He IS!" Shmedley snapped. "He's VERY smart!"

Before the tension could escalate, another group of fans clamored around Hare Pierre, pleading for autographs. The rabbit obliged, his pen gliding across albums and posters.

"You're famous," Doggie marveled.

"Of course I'm famous," Hare Pierre replied. "My love songs are *très* popular."

"Ooh!" said Doggie. "Do you know a lot about love?"

"Yes, naturally," said Hare Pierre, pausing to sign a copy of his album *Extraordinaire* for a starstruck monkey in sparkly glasses. "I know more about love than anyone."

Doggie's eyes lit up. "Great! Can you tell me about it? How do you know when you've found the right person—or, you know, the right animal? I feel like one day I'm going to meet someone perfect for me, and we'll fall in love..."

Hare Pierre frowned. "I thought you were allergic to love. Isn't that one of your stage gimmicks? You sneeze and break out in a rash whenever someone mentions love?"

Doggie laughed. "That's silly! Nobody can be *allergic* to love."

Hare Pierre's frown deepened. "Ah, so it's all a ruse. A clever act. I must say, I'm almost impressed."

Doggie wasn't deterred. "Can you tell me about love?" he pressed.

Hare Pierre smirked. "Love is simple," he declared. "It's when someone adores you more than anything, showers you with gifts, and constantly praises your singing talents and the smell of your cologne."

Doggie tilted his head, confused. "Oh... that's not what I imagined love to be."

Boss interjected. "I wouldn't take love advice from *him*, Mr. Munchabunch."

Hare Pierre raised an eyebrow, looking Boss up and down. "Oh, really? And who are you going to trust for love advice? This old-fashioned salamander?" His gaze lingered. "Though, I must admit, I *do* like your outfit," he added.

Boss nodded graciously. "Why, thank you."

Hare Pierre's fans continued to pester him, pulling him back into their whirlwind of adoration. "Excuse me," he said to Doggie, "but I have to be off."

"Okay," Doggie replied. "Thanks for the advice."

They watched as Hare Pierre strutted away, his entourage trailing after him.

"Okay," said Boss, heaving a heavy sigh. "Hopefully we don't interact with TOO many others..."

Shmedley's eyes widened as he saw someone approaching. "Oh no," he said.

Myrrh was coming.

"Hide!" said Boss, but there was nowhere to hide. Instead, the two salamanders turned to the wall and hid their faces. But Doggie just stared at Myrrh, his heart leaping for some reason he couldn't name.

Myrrh saw Doggie and said, "Hey, Doggie."

"Oh, hello!" said Doggie. "What's *your* name?"

"Haha, real funny," said Myrrh.

"No, really. What's your name?"

"That's really rude, Doggie."

"I'm not *trying* to be rude. I just would like to know your name. I've never seen you before, but I feel like I've known you forever..."

"Wow," said Myrrh, and she walked away in a huff.

Boss and Shmedley turned around. "Why was that pika mad at me?" Doggie asked, looking forlorn.

"It's a long story," said Boss. "We don't have time for it now. I hope Mr. Tomfoolery has finished his business. He's been gone an awfully long time."

"Maybe we should peek in on him," suggested Shmedley.

They opened the door and stepped into Whisker's room, their eyes immediately drawn to a towering, buzzing machine. It was a mesmerizing contraption, covered with flashing lights, glowing knobs, and a tangled mess of wires. The air was thick with the hum of electric energy.

Whisker stood in front of the machine, holding several glass vials in his paws, a distant and melancholy look in his eyes. Boss cleared his throat. "Mr. Tomfoolery?" he asked gently. "Are you all right?"

Whisker blinked, as if waking from a trance. "Huh? Oh. Here," he said, handing the vials of azidozide to Boss.

"Thank you," Boss replied, quickly passing the vials to Shmedley. "These should do the trick. Now, we need to leave immediately. Especially you, Mr. Tomfoolery. You *cannot* be here when your counterpart returns. Seeing yourself could have... well, dire consequences."

Whisker didn't respond. His eyes drifted back to the buzzing, blinking machine. Doggie followed his gaze. "What *is* that thing?" he asked.

Whisker sighed. "The Zabribulator," he said. "My worst—and most awfulest—invention."

"The Zabribulator," Boss echoed, a note of awe in his voice. "Of course."

Whisker's shoulders slumped. "This is what makes Pinkie disappear," he said, his voice heavy with guilt.

"Who's Pinkie?" Doggie asked.

"Never mind that now, Mr. Munchabunch," Boss interrupted. "Yes, Mr. Tomfoolery, the Zabribulator *is* how Pinkie disappears. And we must *let* that event occur. If we change it, everything will unravel."

Whisker's eyes flashed with desperation. "I could dismantle it right now," he said. "Stop Pinkie from disappearing!"

Boss's expression grew stern. "You are a man of science," he reminded him.

Whisker gave a rueful smile. "I'm more like a rat of mischief."

"Yes, but you are also a rat of science," Boss insisted. "You know the rules of time travel. Do you really want to risk unraveling reality itself by meddling with the past?"

Whisker hesitated, his eyes flickering between Boss and the Zabribulator.

"Who's the Special Boo?" said Doggie quietly.

Boss and Shmedley jumped, trembling with fear.

"Sorry," said Doggie. "Sorry. That was me, that time."

"Wait a minute," said Whisker, his eyes lighting up with sudden determination. "ZAP me with the Zabribulator! Make *me* disappear!"

"We can't do that!" Boss protested, looking horrified.

"I'm supposed to be dead right now anyway, dissolved into dreamstuff," said Whisker. "You guys saved me, gave me a second chance. But if you zap me now, maybe I'll end up wherever Pinkie went. I could help her when she gets there." He nodded firmly. "Yes. This is the way to set things right."

Boss and Shmedley exchanged a long, uncertain look.

Doggie glanced anxiously at the door. "What should we do?" he asked. "Shouldn't we hurry? The other Whisker could come back any minute..."

Boss sighed. "Mr. Tomfoolery, the truth is... you were supposed to die, not just disappear."

Whisker clenched his fists. "I don't want to just go off and DIE somewhere! This way is better. If I disappear, I might actually be able to help Pinkie. Maybe I can make things right."

Shmedley nodded slowly, glancing at Boss. "He *would* be out of the timeline that way..."

"All right," Boss said at last. "Fine." He turned to Doggie. "See, Mr. Munchabunch? *That* is love... Mr. Tomfoolery is willing to face the unknown, to risk everything, to fix a mistake and save someone he cares about."

"Oh," said Doggie. "THAT seems more like it."

Whisker twiddled with his backpack straps, looking uncomfortable. "Wait a minute, don't get the wrong idea! I'm not in LOVE with Pinkie!"

Shmedley shrugged. "Sounds like it."

Boss nodded at Whisker. "Okay, Mr. Tomfoolery. We'll zap you."

"Thanks," said Whisker, moving to stand in front of a long copper rod. "When you're ready, press that orange button."

Doggie's ears drooped, and he gave Whisker a sad look. "It was nice getting to know you a little bit, Mr. Tomfoolery."

Whisker chuckled, shaking his head. "I still can't get over the fact that you call me that," he said.

Without warning, Shmedley raised the Thingumybob and zapped Whisker. A dazed, glassy-eyed expression clouded Whisker's face.

"Why'd you do THAT?" Doggie cried, looking shocked.

Shmedley shrugged, his expression somber. "So he won't remember any of this adventure," he explained. "It's better that way."

Boss took a deep breath, then reached for the orange button. With a final glance at Whisker, he pressed it. A blinding bolt of silver lightning burst from the copper rod, crackling and illuminating the room. In an instant, Whisker vanished, as if he'd never been there at all.

CHAPTER 12

BirdSanktuary-Land

BOSS, SHMEDLEY, AND DOGGIE left Whisker's workshop and made their way through the winding streets toward the front entrance of Crisscross Applesauce. The bustling campus was alive with activity, but Doggie's thoughts seemed far away. "I feel bad for that pretty pika we saw earlier," he said.

"Is *that* what Myrrh is?" Shmedley asked. "A pika?"

"Myrrh?" Doggie echoed, his eyes lighting up. "Is *that* her name? She seemed really nice. I can't stop thinking about her. If I ever see her again, I'll make sure to apologize. I really hope I get to see her again... She makes me feel like I have butterflies in my belly."

Boss cleared his throat. "Yes, well," he said. "For now, Mr. Munchabunch, let's focus on getting out of this mountain before you're recognized by anyone else."

They pushed through the crowded town square, weaving around singing animals and lively artists at work. Suddenly, a voice rang out across the park. "Doggie! Hey! What are you doing?"

Doggie turned and saw Kitty Karate waving at him from across the crowd, her voice cutting through the noise. "Doggie!" she called again. "Where are you going? We have band practice in a little while!"

"Don't engage with that cat!" Boss hissed, keeping his head low. He and Shmedley exchanged a glance, then quickly nudged Doggie forward, urging him along before he could respond.

Doggie managed a quick wave. "Uh, hello!" he called back to Kitty, but Boss and Shmedley hurried him forward.

"Doggie, where are you going?" Kitty called again, her voice fading as they moved further away.

Boss and Shmedley kept Doggie moving, guiding him swiftly out of the mountain and back toward the safety of the *Paradox*.

"Who *was* that cat?" Doggie asked.

"That cat is Doggie Cornelius Munchabunch the Third's best friend. She thought *you* were *him*."

"The *Third*?" said Doggie, smiling. "Wow. So, my grandson?"

"No," said Boss. "Just a third animal with that name."

"Oh."

Shmedley got to work refilling the time travel cells with azidozide. Meanwhile, Boss grimly examined the damaged parts of the cockpit. There were jagged shards of glass everywhere, from the shattered windshield.

"We'll need to reshape the spare rear windows and get them in place before the azidozide cells are fully activated," said Boss, already making a list of necessary steps. Shmedley nodded, retrieving two spare rear windows from the emergency compartment.

Both salamanders knew that these windows, originally designed for the back of the *Paradox*, weren't a perfect fit for the cockpit's wide, curved opening. Boss held up the first window, assessing the shape. "Right," he said. "We'll have to meld and reconfigure these to make a proper seal."

Shmedley pulled the Thingumybob out from his inner pocket. Doggie watched in quiet wonder. "Can the Thingumybob really fix the window?"

Shmedley nodded. "Hopefully! There are settings for melding and reshaping."

"Oh," said Doggie. "Won't you also need to use a dash of temporal stabilization, too?"

Boss and Shmedley stopped to stare at him in wonder. "Actually," said Shmedley, "that's not a bad idea."

"Indeed not," agreed Boss. "Here, Mr. Munchabunch, help me hold this spare window steady."

Shmedley adjusted the dials on the Thingumybob. With a soft whir, a controlled beam of white light pulsed over the window's edges. The glass glowed as it softened and became pliable, and Boss used a shaping tool to deftly mold the window into the correct curvature.

"Hold it steady!" Boss instructed, and Doggie obeyed. The window seemed to shimmer like liquid, bending slowly and finally locking into place with a perfect contour that matched the front windshield's frame.

Next, they repeated the process with the second spare window.

At last, both windows were secured into the frame. Boss ran a sensor scan to check for gaps or imperfections, and when the results came back clean, he sighed with relief. To finish the repairs, Shmedley sealed the edges with a bonding agent that glowed briefly before solidifying into a transparent, nearly unbreakable barrier.

"Repairs complete," Boss declared, giving Shmedley and Doggie a proud nod. The *Paradox's* cockpit was once again airtight and stable, and the time travel cells hummed with energy, ready for their next journey.

৩

"SO," SAID DOGGIE, "WHERE to next, Boss?"

Boss adjusted his hat and prepared to launch into his mission briefing. "Alright, our next assignment—"

"We should go to BirdSanktuary-land!" Doggie interrupted. "That's where Shmedley's always wanted to go."

"But we have more pressing matters—" Boss began, only for Doggie to cut him off again.

"Oh, come on," Doggie insisted. "You two have all the time in the world! You're time travelers, for crying out loud!"

Boss let out a long sigh. "I *suppose*," he said, "we could take a quick detour to BirdSanktuary-land. Just a short visit to see what's there."

"Ohhhh!" Shmedley's face lit up in pure joy, his smile so wide it looked like it might split his face in half. "I can't wait!" He dashed off to the back of the ship to grab something.

Boss watched him go, then turned to Doggie with a disapproving look. "You know," he said, "you really shouldn't encourage him. This isn't important work."

"It's important to *him*," Doggie replied simply.

A moment later, Shmedley came bounding back into the cockpit, clutching a blank journal to his chest. "With any luck," he beamed, "I might fill up the rest of my old journal with observations today—and then I'll need this new one!"

Boss sighed. "Fine, fine. What time period should we visit?"

Shmedley's eyes sparkled with excitement. "Oh, it doesn't really matter!" he exclaimed. "ANY period in BirdSanktuary-land would be wonderful! We could even go right now; we don't have to time travel at all!"

Boss rolled his eyes as he pressed buttons and pulled levers. "All right then. Off we go."

With a flick of a switch, Boss activated the cloaking device, making the *Paradox* invisible. The ship rose smoothly into the air, leaving Crisscross Applesauce behind. They soared over the treetops, heading southeast, past Fenmire—where Reversa had once resided—and into the unexplored country of BirdSanktuary-land. Below them lay a breathtaking landscape: dense forests, swamps, lush grassy meadows, and craggy, windswept bluffs.

Shmedley quivered with excitement. "What a wide variety of landscapes!" he breathed. "Just think of all the species we'll discover!"

"Why is this place a sanctuary?" Doggie asked. "Who made it that way?"

"Actually, no one knows for sure," Boss replied. "It's simply the name given to this land. No Stick People, Slurkwyrms, Meemies, or Talking Animals have ever lived here. It's universally understood that this region is meant to be a refuge for wild creatures."

"Especially birds," Shmedley added reverently.

The *Paradox* descended gently, landing on a dry patch of grass near a vernal pool. The three of them stepped out cautiously. All around them, birds sang a lively chorus, their songs weaving through the trees and the reeds.

"Oooh, listen!" said Shmedley. "A beige bunting!"

"We hear those everywhere," said Boss.

"I know, but it *is* my favorite bird," said Shmedley. He wrote down the observation in his journal. Then he looked up, eyes full of hope. "I'm hoping we find a frail nightjar. They are supposed to have the most beautiful songs." Then he froze a moment as a new bird call echoed from the nearby copse of trees. It was a sad, mournful call. It actually made Doggie's heart ache a little bit.

"What was that?" he asked.

Shmedley was shaking so much from excitement, he could barely hold the pencil steady to write in his journal. His eyes had tears in them. "That was the dark-eyed chicoine. Its songs are so sad that it often makes Camsu children cry."

"What are Kam Sue children?" asked Doggie.

"That's the proper name of the Sumac-Tree Stick People," said Boss, trying not to yawn. "They live in nearby Fenmire."

Shmedley kept scribbling in his journal. Nobody said anything for a long time.

At last Boss cleared his throat. "Yes, well. We have observed enough bird species, wouldn't you say?"

Doggie said, "We just got here!" at the same time Shmedley said, "We barely scratched the surface!"

"But nothing of *historical* interest ever happened out here," said Boss.

"True," said Shmedley. "But stuff of *biological* interest happens out here."

Shmedley spent the rest of the day exploring BirdSanktuary-land, notebook in hand, carefully observing the wide array of bird species. As twilight deepened into night, he decided to sleep outside under the vast, starlit sky. Doggie chose to stay with him, while Boss retreated into the *Paradox* to rest comfortably on his cot.

Lying on their backs in the soft grass, Doggie and Shmedley listened to the sounds of the night creatures. The air was alive with the hum of insects and the occasional rustling of unseen wildlife. Around midnight, a hauntingly beautiful, liquid trill drifted through the darkness—a bird song so otherworldly it seemed to hang in the air like a magic spell.

"That's it!" Shmedley whispered, quivering with excitement. "The frail nightjar!" He pointed eagerly toward a nearby sycamore tree. "Look!"

Doggie squinted into the branches and spotted the source of the ethereal music: a stunning bird with silvery plumage, perched on a high branch and singing its enchanting song. "Wow," Doggie breathed.

"I'm so excited to finally see one of those!" Shmedley whispered, barely able to contain his joy.

Doggie smiled warmly. "I like that you love birds so much, Shmedley."

Shmedley turned to him with a grateful grin. "Thank you," he said softly. "They *are* wonderful, aren't they?"

THE NEXT DAY, SHMEDLEY continued his observations. They took the *Paradox* to various parts of BirdSanktuary-land. They explored a rocky bluff, where ground birds scurried among the stones, and then ventured to a swampy section of the forest, where even more bird species awaited. Shmedley's notebook was nearly full, each page bursting with sketches and notes.

As they meandered near the edge of the swamp, a distinctive bird call echoed through the humid air. Shmedley's ears perked up. "Ooh, that's a yellow-headed newtcatcher, I believe," he whispered.

Boss raised an eyebrow. "That sounds... kind of dangerous, Shmedley."

Shmedley nodded. "Well, it *does* feed on newts and salamanders," he admitted. "But I *really* want to see it."

Boss frowned. "Be careful, Shmedley," he cautioned, as his friend crept forward.

Shmedley moved carefully through the towering cattails, inching toward the source of the haunting bird song.

As soon as Shmedley was out of sight, Doggie turned to Boss and said, "Why are you so dismissive of Shmedley's interests?"

Boss blinked, surprised. "I'm not dismissive of Shmedley's hobbies. It's just that we have an important mission, you see."

"Who gave you the mission?" Doggie asked.

"Well, I guess we were born with it," said Boss. "You could say it's our destiny to explore the history of Magic Woods and record our observations for posterity."

"Yeah," said Doggie, "but Shmedley really is happy here. Couldn't we stay a couple more days?"

"I'm afraid not," said Boss. "It's past time for us to go, Mr. Munchabunch."

"But Shmedley has just barely begun to explore this land!" said Doggie. "He discovered three new species already! Who knows how many more are out there?"

Suddenly, Shmedley's joyous yelps rang out across the swamp. "I see it! I see it!" he shouted. "And now my first journal is complete!"

Doggie and Boss pushed through the swamp weeds, making their way toward Shmedley's voice. When they emerged from the dense greenery, they found him dancing happily on a muddy bank, holding his filled notebook triumphantly above his head. He beamed when he saw them. "Look!" he exclaimed, pointing eagerly.

Doggie and Boss peered through the reeds and spotted a large songbird with a striking yellow head, perched delicately on a cattail stem.

"It's the yellow-headed newtcatcher!" Shmedley cried.

"Hooray!" Doggie cheered.

"Yes, hooray," said Boss. "Now, let's get going—"

But before they could take another step, the newtcatcher cocked its head, its bright eyes locking onto Shmedley. It flexed its wings with sudden intensity.

"Look out!" Doggie shouted.

"Behind you!" yelled Boss.

Shmedley barely had time to turn around before the bird launched itself off the cattail. With a swift, predatory dive, it snatched Shmedley in its beak and carried him back to the stem.

Doggie and Boss watched, frozen in horror.

"Oh no!" Boss cried, his eyes wide with disbelief. "I can see him being swallowed! I see his tail disappearing down the bird's throat!"

The yellow-headed newtcatcher swallowed Shmedley in one swift gulp, then flitted away, vanishing into another part of the swamp, leaving only stunned silence in its wake.

The Special Boo

BOSS AND DOGGIE STOOD speechless, gaping at the cattail where the yellow-headed newtcatcher had just swallowed their dear friend.

"I... I can't believe this," Boss murmured at last, his voice cracking with despair. "I can't live without Shmedley." He pulled a little handkerchief from his coat pocket and dabbed at his eyes. "Oh, dear me, I'm going to dry up, I'm crying so much. I can't live without Shmedley! Why didn't I listen to him? Why didn't I let him come to BirdSanktuary-land as many times as he wanted? What's wrong with me?" His knees buckled, and he fell into the mud, sobbing uncontrollably.

Doggie knelt beside him, patting his back gently. His own eyes were filled with tears. "It's okay," he said, trying to muster some hope. "Hey... you know what? We can save him. We can go back in time and save him."

Boss shook his head, sniffing miserably. "No," he whispered. "We can't do that."

From somewhere in the distance, a ghostly voice echoed, *"Who's the Special Boo?"*

Boss shivered. "See?" he said, his voice thick with sorrow. "Just talking about it has summoned the Special Boo. We can't change the past like that."

Doggie didn't give up. "Just one more time," he urged. "Let's mess with the past one last time. Come on, Boss. We *have* to save Shmedley!"

Boss buried his face in his handkerchief. "I don't think it's even possible," he sobbed. "You don't understand. The forces of the future... or the past... or whatever you want to call them—they're strong. The timeline resists change. Especially something as big as saving someone's life. The timeline will fight us. It always fights."

"We saved Whisker," Doggie insisted. "We can do it again. We *have* to try, Boss."

For a moment, Boss was silent. Then, all at once, he stood up straight, determination flaring in his eyes. He wiped the mud from his knees and tucked his soggy handkerchief back into his pocket. "All right," he said, his voice steady. "Let's do it."

Without another moment's hesitation, they raced into the *Paradox* and began pressing buttons, ready to defy time itself to bring their friend back.

ↄ৲

THEY TRAVELED BACK IN time to just a few minutes before Shmedley's death. "Be careful," Boss whispered as he and Doggie stepped cautiously out of the *Paradox*. "We mustn't be seen by our past selves."

"What are we going to do?" Doggie asked. "What's the plan?"

"We have to grab Shmedley before the bird strikes," Boss explained. "Remember, the past you and I never saw the exact moment when the bird grabbed him. We only saw the bird swallowing him once it returned to the cattail. So, if we can reach Shmedley right before the attack, our past selves will be none the wiser. At least... that's the plan."

Ahead, they saw Shmedley joyfully dancing beside the swamp, shouting, "I see it! And now my first journal is complete!"

"Okay," said Boss. "Let's slink over there and get into position."

But as they tried to approach, it felt like they were wading through thick syrup. The air seemed to solidify around them, and every movement became painfully slow, as if time itself resisted their interference.

"*Who's the Special Boo!?*" an ominous voice called behind them, louder and more menacing than ever.

Doggie tried to yell, "Shmedley! Don't go any closer to that newtcatcher!" But his voice was swept away by a sudden gust of wind, vanishing into the thick air.

Shmedley continued scribbling in his journal, completely unaware of the danger.

Doggie and Boss tried shouting again, but their voices were muffled and distorted, as if being smothered by an invisible force. The struggle against the syrupy air was exhausting, and their panic began to rise.

"It really *is* hard to change the past," Doggie said. "What are we going to do?"

"Keep trying!" Boss urged.

They fought to inch closer, but the mud clung to their feet, the air pressed against them, and their minds felt foggy and sluggish. Helplessly, they watched as the newtcatcher cocked its head, poised to strike.

"Oh no!" Boss cried, desperately trying to free his foot from the mud. "We're going to have to watch it happen all over again!"

In a moment of desperation, Doggie scooped up a clump of mud. *Grace of Good Luck,* he silently prayed, *please let this work.* Drawing on every ounce of luck he could muster (the luck Saffron Friday had gifted him), he hurled the mud with all his strength.

His aim was terrible. The mud didn't hit the bird—it didn't even come close. But it *did* hit Shmedley squarely in the face, knocking him down just as the bird lunged. The newtcatcher missed Shmedley and, instead, snatched a wild salamander that had been swimming nearby. With its prize in its beak, the bird returned to the cattail and swallowed the salamander whole.

From a distance, Doggie and Boss could hear the Boss of the past crying out, "Oh no! I can see him being swallowed! I see his tail going down the bird's throat!"

But in reality, Shmedley was lying flat on the muddy ground, covered in muck. He lifted his head, dazed, and wiped off the mud. Then he spotted the *other* Boss and Doggie staring at him. They pressed their fingers to their lips, signaling him to stay silent. Shmedley, confused but obedient, nodded.

Once the past versions of Boss and Doggie left for the *Paradox*, Boss and Doggie motioned for Shmedley to come over. The air no longer felt thick, and the fog lifted from their minds.

Shmedley stumbled toward them, looking bewildered. "What are you guys doing over here?" he asked. "I thought you were behind me just a moment ago. I'm so confused..."

Boss pulled Shmedley into a tight embrace, tears streaming down his face. "Oh, Shmedley, my dear, dear Shmedley," he sobbed. "Oh, how I love you."

Shmedley blinked, completely lost. "Huh?"

"It's a long story," Doggie said, wiping away tears of relief and wrapping his arms around them both.

"Who's the Special Boo!?" called the voice, louder than ever.

Boss, Shmedley, and Doggie spun around in terror. They could SEE the Special Boo now. He was a rotund, unsettling creature with three eyes. Two of his eyes were enormous, swirling and hypnotic, while the third eye, centered on his forehead, was all-seeing and fixed directly on them.

The Special Boo's middle eye widened impossibly, and his gaping mouth stretched open as he bellowed again, "WHO'S THE SPECIAL BOO!?"

"Quick!" Boss shouted. "Into the *Paradox*!"

They scrambled into the ship, their hands shaking as they punched buttons and pulled levers. But the time circuits flickered and failed, refusing to respond.

"Oh no," Boss moaned. "We've meddled with time too much. Now we're in serious trouble."

Boss and Shmedley frantically worked the controls, but nothing seemed to work. Meanwhile, Doggie peered out the window, his heart pounding as he saw the Special Boo lumbering closer, each step shaking the ground. "He's coming!" Doggie cried. "He's coming!"

"WHO'S THE SPECIAL BOO!!??"

The voice was deafening, reverberating through the *Paradox*, causing the entire ship to shudder.

"This is horrible!" Boss shouted in panic. "How are we ever going to get out of here?"

Doggie scratched his head, a sudden thought striking him. "Wait—just because the time circuits aren't working, does that mean the main thrusters won't work? We could fly away to a different *place*, even if we can't jump to another *time*."

Shmedley's eyes lit up. "That's a great idea!"

"It just might work," said Boss.

Shmedley quickly adjusted the controls and pressed a new set of buttons. For a tense moment, the *Paradox* refused to budge, its engines sputtering. The Special Boo loomed closer, his mouth gaping wide as if preparing to swallow them whole. The sky above twisted and warped ominously.

But then, with a roar, the *Paradox's* main thrusters kicked into life. The ship lurched upward, and they rocketed into the sky, leaving the Special Boo behind in a cloud of dust.

"We did it!" Doggie cheered.

"Yes," said Boss. "But he'll be back. He's never gotten this close to us before. I don't know if anywhere—or *anywhen*—is safe for us anymore."

CHAPTER 14

Stranger Things Have Happened

THEY LANDED IN THE dark forest behind Figgy Pudding about half an hour later. The *Paradox* settled quietly among the trees. In the back room, Doggie slept soundly.

Boss and Shmedley stepped outside the vehicle, leaving Doggie to his sleep. "Thank you for saving my life," said Shmedley after Boss recounted the events of their adventure. "But... I'm afraid of the Special Boo. Do you think he's going to come for us?"

"Of that, I have no doubt," said Boss.

Shmedley swallowed hard. "Why do you think the time circuits aren't working anymore?"

Boss sighed. "I know *exactly* why," he replied. "The Special Boo is too close to us. It must be because we saved you when you were meant to die. The timeline doesn't like to be changed... and I think the Special Boo is going to make sure we never do it again."

A brilliant light appeared above the trees, casting long shadows in the forest. A gentle humming sound filled the air: *"Mm-MM-mm."*

Shmedley raised a hand to shield his eyes from the light. "Boss," he whispered, "what *is* that? Is that... is that..."

Boss's eyes widened, and he spoke softly, almost reverently. "I think it is. I think it's the goddess Ma'ama."

The light shone on them, and a voice, sweet and musical, echoed from the sky. *"Mm-MM,"* said Ma'ama. *"The Special Boo is coming after you and will overtake you very soon."*

"Is there ANY way we can outrun him?" Boss asked.

"You can't, in the long run," Ma'ama answered. *"Mm-MM, but you still have a little time... if you fix something."*

"What do we need to fix?" Boss asked.

Above, the sky twisted and churned, the very fabric of reality shuddering as if strained. The world around them glitched, like a fractured illusion.

"Mm-MM, Doggie was supposed to disappear, and he hasn't."

Shmedley's voice trembled. "But why does it matter? There's going to be other Doggies."

"They are all the same Doggie."

"What?" said Shmedley.

"Mm-MM, he returns in the same form, two more times. Mm-MM-mm. And if this version does not disappear SOON, so he can come back in his other incarnations, it will spell disaster for this world and many others."

Shmedley's heart sank. "Well, what are we supposed to do about that *now*?" he asked helplessly. "He's our friend. He's part of our team."

Before Ma'ama could answer, they heard a familiar voice. Doggie had woken up and stepped outside, and they hadn't even noticed him approach. "So," Doggie said, looking up at the radiant figure in the sky, "flying light-bulb lady, you mean I have to disappear, or the whole world's gonna get destroyed?"

"Yes," said Ma'ama.

"No!" Shmedley cried, tears springing to his eyes. "We're not going to let you disappear!"

Doggie's expression was full of sorrow, but he gave a resigned nod. "It's okay," he said softly. "It sounds like I'd better do it. Disappear, that is." He turned to Boss and Shmedley. "But I'm gonna miss you guys. And... I never even got to eat anything. When I come back to the world, I won't be so picky about food."

Shmedley bowed his head, tears streaming down his face. "I'm so sorry," he sobbed.

Doggie took a deep breath, his heart aching. "Will I be able to remember everything that happened?" he asked Ma'ama.

"*Mm, no,*" she said gently. "*You must not remember this incarnation.*"

Doggie's ears drooped. "Oh," he whispered. "That's sad." He straightened up, summoning all the courage he had. "But... I *have* to do it. To save the world."

Ma'ama floated up and away, disappearing into the starry sky. "*Farewell animals, and good luck!*" she said.

Doggie looked at Boss. "Well, how are you guys gonna make me disappear? Are you gonna zap me with the Thingumybob?"

"No," said Shmedley miserably. "We don't have a setting for that."

"Wait!" said Boss. "The Black Hole of Flowerfield. If something falls in there, they eventually disappear."

Doggie swallowed nervously. "I need to fall into a big black hole?"

"Yes," said Boss. "I think that's the only way."

Doggie began to shiver. Shmedley touched his arm and said, "Don't worry, it'll all turn out okay in the end."

The sky above began to twist again, like reality was being scrunched. They heard, "*Who's the Special Boo?*" in the distance.

"Okay," said Doggie. "Let's do it."

☙

THEY REACHED FLOWERFIELD A little while later, landing the *Paradox* at the edge of the forest, not far from the ominous Black Hole. Stepping out of the vehicle, they stood before it—a gaping void, darker and colder than the space between stars.

Doggie shivered, trying to steady himself. "Okay, so... what do I have to do? Just, like, jump in?"

"Yes," said Boss. "But first, as Ma'ama instructed, we need to delete all your memories of your time with us."

"Oh. Right."

Boss nodded at his assistant. "All right, Shmedley. Let's... let's do it."

Shmedley lifted the Thingumybob, but his hands were trembling too much to hold it steady. Tears spilled down his face, and he dropped the device, running to Doggie and wrapping him in a desperate hug. "I can't do it!" he sobbed. "I'm going to miss you too much!"

Doggie hugged him back, his voice soft. "I'll miss you too. Maybe someday we'll be together again."

"Unlikely," Boss muttered, "since you won't remember us."

Shmedley shot him a deep, wounded look.

Boss backpedaled. "But, of course," he added quickly, "sometimes the impossible happens. So... you never know."

"Yeah," Shmedley whispered. "You never know."

Boss picked up the Thingumybob. "*I'll* zap him, Shmedley," he said gently. "So you don't have to."

Shmedley nodded, tears still streaming down his face. He gave Doggie one last, heartfelt hug before stepping away.

Doggie took a deep breath, trying to lighten the moment. "Two for Yesterday," he said.

"Huh?" Shmedley asked, wiping his eyes.

Doggie gave a sad smile. "You said you guys didn't have your own story, that you only observed the adventures of others. But I think you *do* have a story. A good one! And I think it should be called *Two for Yesterday*, because, see, there are two of you, and you're always traveling to yesterday... yesterday as in the *past*, not necessarily *literal* yesterday, as in the day before right now. Argh. You know what I mean."

Shmedley managed a tearful smile. "*Two for Yesterday*. I like that. I only wish it could have been *Three for Yesterday*."

Doggie nodded sadly. "For a little while, it was."

Boss fiddled nervously with the Thingumybob, adjusting knobs and muttering under his breath. "Do you need help, Boss?" Shmedley asked, his voice still thick with sadness.

"No, no, I've got it," Boss insisted, though his hands were shaking. "I'm a scientist, after all. I co-created this thing."

"Okay," Shmedley whispered.

Finally, Boss stepped back, taking a steadying breath. "All right, Mr. Munchabunch. Ready?"

Doggie's voice was quiet. "I guess so."

Boss activated the Thingumybob, and waves of colored light pulsed out, the most powerful blast Shmedley had ever seen. The light washed over Doggie, and his face went blank, as though his mind had been wiped completely clean. He stumbled backward, dazed, and fell into the Black Hole, vanishing from sight.

Shmedley turned away, unable to bear it.

Boss stared down at the Thingumybob. "I... I might have zapped him a little too hard with the memory scrambler. Worst case scenario, he could become the opposite of who he's meant to be."

Shmedley wiped at his eyes, his voice bitter. "Oh, so instead of *wanting* to fall in love, he'll be *allergic* to it?"

Boss shifted uncomfortably. "Well... yes. That *could* happen."

"And instead of being a picky eater, he'll eat just about everything?"

Boss nodded. "Um, yes, that's another *possible* side effect."

"And he'll be scared, not brave? And maybe not so scientifically-minded?"

Boss sighed. "Sure, sure, those effects could all happen—*if* I had blasted him too hard. But... regardless. We did what needed to be done."

They looked up. The sky above had settled, no longer twisting, and the air felt calm, free of the glitchy, ominous tension that had plagued it.

Shmedley started to cry again.

"Remember, Shmedley, he'll come back in a new body," said Boss. "Twice, apparently."

"But he'll never remember us, Boss."

Boss touched Shmedley's arm. "Well, you never know. Stranger things have happened."

જ

BOSS AND SHMEDLEY RETURNED to Laterberry alone, the *Paradox* landing with a quiet sigh amidst the juniper trees.

They stepped into the mountain with slumped shoulders. The silence of the empty rooms felt heavier than ever. Wordlessly, Shmedley took out the Thingumybob and held it in his trembling hands. With a heavy sigh, he adjusted the probability parameters and tried to summon some dinner. He pressed the button, but only a pile of stale crackers tumbled onto the floor, dry and unappetizing.

Shmedley stared at them, his lip quivering. "I can't even summon plum pudding," he said, his voice barely above a whisper. He pushed the crackers away, and they scattered across the floor like so many broken promises.

"It's all right, old friend," Boss said gently, sitting beside him. "Let's get out of this lonely mountain and take a walk. Maybe the fresh air will do us some good."

Together, they stepped out of Laterberry and wandered through the forest, the night air cool and sweet. The stars above were bright and infinite, scattered like silver jewels across the sky. They walked in silence for a while, the only sounds the rustling of leaves and the occasional call of a night bird.

Shmedley didn't even reach for his journal when he heard the birdsong.

"Er," said Boss hesitantly. "What species of bird was that, do you think?"

104

Shmedley shrugged. "I dunno."

"*Mm-MM-mm.*" Then, all at once, Ma'ama appeared above them again. "*You have fixed what was wrong. Your time circuits should be working again.*"

"Excellent!" said Boss. "And the Special Boo?"

"*Mm-MM, you have outrun him... for now.*"

"Good," said Boss, breathing a sigh of relief.

"*But not forever. Now that the Special Boo has seen you, he will follow you everywhere until, at last, he swallows you whole.*"

"Great," said Shmedley. "Our destiny is to be devoured by a three-eyed time monster."

"*The only safe place,*" Ma'ama continued, "*is the Forest in the Sky.*"

"But we can't go there," said Boss.

"*I can bring you there, when the time is right.*"

"Wow," Shmedley breathed. "Really?"

"*Mm-MM, yes. But first, I have a couple of missions for you.*"

Boss's eyes lit up. "Missions? Yes! Oh, please, give us some missions!"

"*Mm-MM, you must document as many wild bird species as you can. ALL of them, if possible.*"

Boss's jaw dropped. "Say what?"

Shmedley's whole demeanor changed. His eyes shone with excitement. "Really? I'm way ahead of you, Ms. Ma'ama! I already have one notebook full of observations."

"*Mm-MM, that is good. And when the Special Boo draws close again, as he surely will, I can lift you up to the Forest in the Sky, where you may dwell in peace and happiness forever.*"

"Thank you, Ma'ama!" said Shmedley, saluting her light.

"*Mm-MM, oh, and just before you come to my world, be sure to grab me a croissant from Four & Twenty Blackbirds. I've always wanted to know what those taste like.*"

Shmedley nodded. "As you wish!"

"Mm-MM, farewell, salamanders, and good luck!" They watched as Ma'ama drifted away into the night sky.

Shmedley turned to Boss with an apologetic look. "I'm sorry, Boss, that our missions involve bird-watching now."

Boss smiled and squeezed Shmedley's shoulder. "That's perfectly fine, my good friend. You've earned it." He took off his spectacles and polished them thoughtfully. "And, you know, just so we're *both* happy, perhaps we can search for the birds near ancient ruins, or active battlefields, or sites of historic importance?"

Shmedley's smile widened. "We'll see," he said.

THE ORIGINAL "MAGIC WOODS" SERIES
The Pumpkin of Magic Woods
The Lost Crowns of Magic Woods
The Last Days of Magic Woods

MAGIC WOODS ADVENTURES
Friends of the Disappeared
Three for Yesterday

LEGENDS OF MAGIC WOODS (PREQUEL SERIES)
The Adventures of Aira
Sisters of the Golden Circle
The Fortunate Four
The Changing of the World
The Lost Kingdom
Forgotten Tales

SEQUEL
The Worlds Beyond Magic Woods

ALSO AVAILABLE
The Complete Guide to Magic Woods
(and the Worlds Beyond)

Listen to the *Magic Woods, Legends of Magic Woods,* and *The World Beyond Magic Woods* podcasts on Spotify, Apple Podcasts, Audible, Google Podcasts, and other platforms.

Visit magic-woods.net for more information!

Made in the USA
Las Vegas, NV
18 December 2024

14722733R00069